DARK WOODS

STEVE VOAKE

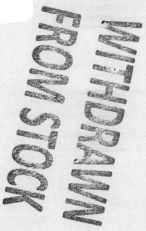

ff

faber and faber

First published in the United Kingdom in 2011
by Faber and Faber Limited
Bloomsbury House
74–77 Great Russell Street
London WC1B 3DA

Printed in England by CPI Bookmarque, Croydon

The right of Steve Voake to be identified as author of this work
has been asserted in accordance with Section 77 of the Copyright,
Designs and Patents Act 1988

A CIP record for this book
is available from the British Library

ISBN 978–0–571–26005–8

2 4 6 8 10 9 7 5 3 1

ONE

Cal was discovered outside Pizza Hut in a blue hold-all with the zip three-quarters done up, which showed his mum cared enough to make sure he didn't get cold. She had put in a brown, threadbare blanket, a book of nursery rhymes and a note which said: *Im sorry I cant do it no more. Pleese look after him. His name is Cal.*

The old man who found him took him to Camden police station, probably hoping for some kind of reward. But rewards were for the things that people actually wanted, so the old man went away empty-handed and Cal lay on his brown blanket in a draughty police station, staring at the ceiling and waiting for his life to begin.

Thirteen years later he was travelling across America in the back of a rented camper van, taken on holiday by the latest in a long line of foster parents, drawing pictures in his notebook and keeping his usual distance from a world that never wanted him in the first place.

'Sketching the scenery, Cal?' asked Sarah, the woman who had spent the last six months trying to be his mother, although they both knew she wasn't succeeding.

Cal nodded, but didn't reply. She had obviously thought a trip to the States might bring them closer together and he could tell she was upset by the fact that this morning, like every other morning, he had got up early and eaten his breakfast alone.

'It would be so nice if just for once we could start the day as a family,' she had said as he washed and dried his bowl before returning it to the cupboard. 'Don't you think, Cal?'

But Cal had heard that kind of talk before. He had even been taken in by it once or twice before learning that there was only one person he could rely upon to look after Cal, and that was Cal. What was the point in trying to complicate things when you knew how they were going to end?

As Sarah turned back to ask Michael *How far is it now?* Cal finished shading the man's jacket and returned the pencil to the pencil case before flipping back through the pages. All the drawings were exactly the same. A man with a pale, white face dressed in a green frock coat and top hat, holding a pair of scissors from which blood dripped to form a dark red pool beneath his feet.

Cal closed the notebook and stared out of the window at a sign which read

West Fork Campground, Bitterroot River
RV Park & Riverside Camping
75 spaces

'You look pale, Cal,' said Michael, glancing in his rear-view mirror. 'Are you feeling OK?'

Cal nodded.

He watched the mountains scratch their silhouettes across the sky, shadows deepening beneath the pine trees as they drove down the forest track.

He didn't know it, of course, but he was only hours away from the meeting which would change his life.

Two

Behind the campground, the mountain's steep, tree-covered slopes swept up into a bruised Montana sky. Four hundred feet above the boundary fence, hidden in the shadows of the pines, Jefferson Boyd watched smoke rise from a dozen barbecues and felt his pulse quicken. Taking a deep breath, he concentrated on remaining calm, because experience had taught him that emotions can cloud your judgement and he didn't want to mess things up.

He was a scientist, after all. And good scientists were cool and methodical, eliminating errors and making sure that everything went according to plan.

Through powerful binoculars he watched the families gathering outside their camper vans, carefully arranging their food on individual picnic tables and preparing to settle in for the evening. Jefferson tried to remember what it was like to be part of a family, sharing food and conversation with people who were close to you. But then he clenched his fist and punched himself in the leg, eager for the pain to remind him how foolish it was to think of such things when there was work to be done.

It was oddly exciting to think that, somewhere down there, someone existed who might be able to help him. He didn't know anything about them yet, of course, didn't know what strange winds of fate might have blown them down the highway towards him. But he knew that these things could not be rushed. After all, he had waited over twenty years for this opportunity.

He was prepared to be patient.

Reaching beneath his camouflage jacket, he took the Smith & Wesson .38 from its concealed holster, opened the chamber and inspected the bullets inside.

He hoped he wouldn't have to use them.

But he knew that trouble had a way of coming at you from the places you least expected.

THREE

The site owner told Michael the fish were rainbow trout, line-caught from the river that morning. 'All you gotta do is walk a mile upstream,' he said. 'The water's glittering with 'em.'

Cal watched Michael lay them on the barbecue, the last rays of sunlight illuminating the oily patches of colour beneath their gills as the flames licked around them, turning them charcoal black.

'You should let her make breakfast for you once in a while,' said Michael when Sarah had gone inside to fetch some cutlery. He flipped the trout over and the scales sizzled, flaking onto the coals like metallic rain. 'She only wants to look after you.'

'I can look after myself,' said Cal.

'I know,' said Michael, 'but you don't have to. Not any more.'

Later that night as he lay awake listening to the sound of their breathing, Cal wondered how long it would be before they gave up on him. Called it a day and sent him back to the children's home, just like all the others had done. Families always fostered him for a while, but never adopted, not since that first time. Everyone wanted babies these days, not teenagers who didn't want to be there.

'Boomerang Cal,' that's what they called him. Boomerang Cal – the boy who keeps coming back.

He could see it now. Almost looked forward to it, in fact. The way he would unpack his stuff, hang his clothes in the cheap flat-pack wardrobe and go back to making his own breakfast without anyone bothering him.

He thought about that for a while. Then he closed his eyes and fell asleep.

A blood-red sky giving way to night. The moon hanging low in the treetops and Cal in a place he didn't recognise. A cheap candlewick bedspread and a dusty lampshade throwing shadows across the room. A window and a night full of stars. In the darkness, someone standing in the shadows. Staring at Cal and smiling . . .

As the screams echoed around Cal's mind he struggled from beneath the duvet like a drowning man and Sarah ran through the cabin, knocking pans from the stove in her efforts to get to him.

'It's all right,' she whispered, reaching for his hand in the darkness, 'it was only a dream.'

Cal held her hand for a few moments until the fear subsided. Then, as she put her hand on his shoulder, he turned his face to the wall.

'I'll always be here if you need me, Cal,' she whispered. 'But you have to trust me. You have to let me in.'

Cal wanted to believe it this time. But knowing that if he did the world would only let him down again, he said nothing and closed his eyes. As he drifted off to sleep he felt her lie down beside him, whispering in the darkness:

> Star light, star bright
> First star I see tonight
> I wish I may, I wish I might
> Have the wish I wish tonight

FOUR

Jefferson Boyd sat with his back against a tree and zipped up his fleece. He took three sips from his water bottle and ate a handful of trail mix that he had picked up from the gas station en route. Then he took the night-vision goggles he had got mail order for two hundred dollars and slipped them over his head. As his eyes adjusted, he saw the grey shapes of the rocks and trees, the eerie green heat of birds returning to their nests and the fading glow of barbecue coals.

It looked promising, but he would just have to be patient.

When the time was right, he would make his move.

FIVE

Cal woke early, just as the sun was coming up. Although it was dark inside the camper van, there was still enough light for him to see Sarah lying on the bed next to him. He guessed she must have slept there all night.

Feeling a pang of something he didn't want to feel, Cal immediately shut it down, locking it away so that it couldn't hurt him. Careful not to wake her, he slid past and dressed himself. He took two slices of bread from the bread bin and spread them with butter and jam. Then he opened the door and sat at the picnic table, eating his breakfast and watching the sun come up over the mountains.

He wondered briefly what it would be like to have a mother after all these years, but he knew he couldn't allow himself to think about such things. So he forced the last of the bread down, licked his fingers and wiped his hands on his jeans. There was a bowl next to the table full of last night's washing-up. Although he didn't know why, he suddenly wanted to do something for her. Something that wouldn't involve talking or hoping or believing in promises that couldn't be kept.

He went inside and took some washing-up liquid and a cloth from the drainer. Then he picked up the bowl and walked down the road towards the washrooms. There were a couple of double sinks built into the outside of the block and he filled one with hot water, frothing up the suds before dumping in the plates and cutlery.

'Looks like you know what you're doing,' said a voice. Cal turned to see a girl smiling at him over a pile of plates. She was maybe a year or two older than him, with short red hair and a handful of freckles sprinkled across her nose like pepper dust. 'You wanna do a few more?'

Without waiting for an answer, she placed the plates on the drainer next to his, rolled up her sleeves and turned the taps on full blast.

'I'm telling ya, if I ever have kids I'm going to send 'em out to work while I stay home watching TV and eating Hershey bars.' She dug in her pocket and pulled out a pack of Life Savers. 'Want one? Beats cleaning your teeth.'

'Thanks.' Cal took a mint and saw that she was watching him with interest, trying to figure him out.

'You just got here?'

'Last night.'

'You're English, right?'

'That obvious, is it?'

'Put it this way. The only other place I've heard people talk like you is in the movies. Usually standing next to a horse and carriage.' She smiled. 'It's not a bad thing. I like it.'

'OK. Well . . . good.'

Not knowing what else to say, Cal stuck his hands in the sink and began scrubbing the remains of last night's dinner off the plates.

'Barbecue?'

'Yup.'

'Same. The name's Eden, by the way. As in Garden of.'

'I'm Cal. You live round here?'

'Nah, I'm from Orange County. My dad owns a farm on the coast.' Seeing the blank look on Cal's face, she jerked her thumb over her shoulder and added, 'California. Like, a gazillion miles in that direction.'

She put a plate on the drainer and threw a fistful of cutlery into the sink.

'See, where I come from we're surrounded by

palm trees and I get to hang out with my friends down at the beach. So my dad says, "Ooh, I know – let's take Eden on a road trip for three weeks and see how many boring places we can visit." I'm telling you, there ain't a monument too dull or a museum too dusty that my dad won't want to have his photograph taken next to it.'

Cal smiled, partly because he had never met anyone quite like her, and partly because she knew nothing about him. It was like turning over a fresh page of his notebook; like starting over.

'Why are you up so early, anyways?' She grinned mischievously. 'You pee the bed or something?'

Cal blushed. 'I couldn't sleep.'

'Join the club. Been lying there for hours, thinking about the thousand-mile nature hike he's probably got planned. So I thought I'd get up, make myself useful and see what the day had to offer.'

She dried the last couple of plates, wiped her hands on her jeans and pulled down the sleeves of her sweatshirt.

'How d'you fancy doing a spot of exploring before breakfast?'

Cal followed Eden's gaze to the pine trees that grew from the side of the mountain.

'Now?'

'Why not?' She looked at her watch. 'It's 6 a.m.

and my folks won't be up for a couple of hours yet. But soon as they are, it'll be, "Eden, get yourself ready, we've got some fascinating guidebooks we want you to read." So what do you say? Are you up for it?'

Cal thought of Sarah and Michael, still asleep in the van. He thought of all the places he had lived, of all the people who had come and gone and of how whatever happened always seemed to be decided by someone else.

'OK,' he said, picking up the bowl of crockery. 'I'll just take these back. See you in five minutes.'

Six

Jefferson woke to the sound of birdsong. A pair of nuthatches chattered in the branches and a dove called soft and low as the first rays of sunlight burned off the morning mist. He rolled up his sleeping bag, brushed off the loose bark and tied it beneath his rucksack. He took a swig from his water bottle, rubbed his teeth with the side of his finger and spat into an anthill. He watched them scurry around for a while, trying to figure out how to put the pine needles back together again. Then he raised his binoculars and watched the boy he'd seen the night before walk past the shower block towards the boundary gate. There was a girl with him, which was unfortunate. But he wasn't about to turn back now: if she came along too, then he'd just have to deal with it.

'That's right,' he said softly. 'You just keep on walking.'

He watched the girl unlatch the gate, standing

aside to allow the boy through before following him into the woods and closing the gate behind her. The boy was maybe thirteen or fourteen, the girl a little older. The boy's hair was buzz-cut like he was preparing for the military or something, but generally he didn't seem like the outdoor type. His face was indoor-pale and he was wearing jeans and a dark blue sweatshirt. Jefferson knew he'd feel the heat when the sun came up and guessed he was a city boy, more used to sidewalks and shopping malls, something which would make Jefferson's job a whole lot easier. Turning his attention to the girl, he saw that she was also pale skinned, but that was maybe down to her natural colouring. She seemed to be doing much of the talking, but every now and then the boy would say something which would make her laugh, or stop and shake her head as if to say: *No way, really?*

He guessed they were friends, which might be a problem. But he decided not to dwell upon it.

In his experience, if you looked at trouble long enough, it usually turned into an opportunity.

SEVEN

Cal was warming to Eden, felt as though they were already friends. But it wasn't easy trying to work out what you thought about things while she was around. He was used to being with people who only spoke when they wanted you to do something, to talk about your feelings or, now and again, to call you names before they kicked your head in. But Eden was different. She talked so much that her words tumbled around his brain like clothes in a drier. Before he even had time to peer inside and see whether they were socks or shirts, she would just open up the door and throw a whole new load in.

It was confusing.

But he liked it.

'My dad reckons you can walk the whole of the Rockies on these paths. Says you can go for days without bumping into anyone.' She picked up a stick and swiped at a sage bush by the edge of the trail. 'Amazing, really. Behind us there's TV and tele- phones. In front of us, a thousand square miles of wilderness.'

'That's a lot of wilderness.'

Cal saw a grey squirrel watching him from the trees and stepped off the trail to take a closer look.

'Hey, don't touch that, whatever you do,' said Eden.

'It's just a squirrel,' said Cal. 'What's it going to do? Peanut me to death?'

'Not that. The plants.'

Cal looked down, half-expecting to see some sharp thorns or a patch of stinging nettles, but all he could see were a few shiny green leaves. Although they appeared harmless enough, the look on Eden's face stopped him in his tracks.

'It's poison ivy, Cal. Touch that and you'll blister up like bubble-wrap.'

'What?'

'I'm telling you. A kid in our neighbourhood fell into some once and you could hear his screams from two blocks away. His hand swelled up like a baseball glove and for the next few weeks he had to walk around slathered in lotion.'

'Wow, OK,' said Cal, reversing back onto the path. 'All that from one little plant?'

'You'd better believe it. Don't you have that kind of stuff back home?'

Cal looked at the blue sky and the butterflies dancing above the path in front of him.

'Not really, no.'

He stared at the ivy again, fascinated by the thought of all that pain hidden beneath its innocent green leaves.

'Are you feeling OK?' asked Eden as they carried on up the trail. 'I mean, I hope you don't mind me saying, but you seemed kind of miserable earlier on.'

'Most people are pretty miserable at six in the morning,' said Cal, wondering if all Americans were this direct.

'There's miserable and there's miserable,' said Eden. 'Did you have an argument with your parents or something?'

'They aren't my parents,' said Cal.

The forest hummed with insects, like an electric generator.

'OK,' said Eden. 'Now that *is* interesting.'

Cal could tell that she was intrigued, but he didn't feel like going into it. So he just pointed at a smaller path that branched off into the trees and said, 'Where do you reckon that goes?'

Eden followed his gaze, then pointed with her stick.

'How about we find out?'

EIGHT

Eden gestured for Cal to go first and, after checking for poison ivy, he squeezed through the bushes into the forest. It was incredible really, the difference a few metres could make. While the path had been in the full heat of the sun, the air beneath the trees was cooler and heavier, laden with the scent of pines.

'Are you *sure* this is the way to McDonald's?' asked Eden.

Cal was still trying to think of a witty reply when he heard a voice calling through the trees.

'Tansy? Tansy, where are you? Come on now, stop messing around, will ya?'

Cal leaned against a tree and waited for Eden to catch up with him. Together they stood and listened to the sound of the man's voice, somewhere up ahead.

After a few moments, the voice stopped. Cal heard

the snap of a branch breaking and turned to see a man standing in dappled sunlight beneath the pines. He looked to be somewhere in his mid-forties and was dressed in a check shirt and combat trousers. Draped around his neck was a pair of binoculars and on his back was a canvas rucksack with a sleeping bag tied underneath. He had brown, shoulder-length hair which looked as if it hadn't been washed in a while, and as he ran a hand through it his eyes darted back and forth between the two of them.

'My dog,' he said. 'Have you seen her?'

Cal shook his head.

'Sorry. We only just got here.'

'Are you sure?' The man frowned and scratched the stubble on his chin. 'She came this way less than two minutes ago.'

Cal was surprised at how softly spoken the man was. From his appearance he had expected something harder, less educated. But he knew from the poison ivy that appearances could be deceptive.

'What kind of dog is he?' asked Eden.

'She,' the man corrected her. 'I said that already, didn't I?'

There was an awkward silence for a moment or two, but Eden was quick to fill it.

'We could help you look for her, if you like,' she

offered, throwing a sidelong glance at Cal. 'I mean, it's not like we've got anything else to do, right, Cal?'

'Right,' said Cal. There was something about the man which made him uneasy. Something about the way he kept running his fingers through his hair, like he was nervous about something. But then he had just lost his dog, Cal reasoned. And Cal knew that losing something you cared about could do all kinds to a person.

'Listen,' the man said. 'I think that's her. Did you hear it?'

Cal listened, but all he could hear was the hum of insects and the whisper of the breeze.

'I think I hear it too,' said Eden, and Cal could see that she was enjoying the new direction the morning was taking. 'Come on. Let's go find her.'

She set off through the trees with the man beside her and Cal followed. After a while the path disappeared and Cal found himself pushing through thick branches as he tried to keep up. The muscles in his legs ached and he realised that instead of walking around the base of the mountain as they had been, they were now heading upwards, leaving the path further and further behind.

'You all right back there?' called the man's voice.

'I'm fine,' said Cal.

Although they were now in the shadow of the

pines, the sun was higher and the air warm and humid. Cal pulled his sweatshirt over his head and tied it around his waist. He leaned against a tree, smelling the fragrance of pine needles and watching a line of ants march up the trunk. He wondered what time it was and whether he should be getting back. Maybe he should have left a note. But then, what did it matter? Sarah might want to be his mother, but the truth was she was just one more stop along a very long road. He would move on and forget about her and Michael, same as he always did, and these few weeks would be no more than a distant dream.

'I'm coming,' he said.

When he caught up with them they were waiting on a plateau where the trees thinned out to give a view all the way across the valley to the mountains beyond. A buzzard circled high above them, its jagged calls scratching the sky.

'It's beautiful, don't you think?' said the man. 'The kind of thing dreams are made of.'

Cal thought it was a strange thing to say, but then he guessed he was a strange guy, walking around with his sleeping bag and binoculars.

'Any sign of the dog?'

The man shook his head. 'All I can think is she must have made her way back to the van. Reckon she picked up the scent of a buck rabbit and couldn't resist going after it. But I appreciate you helping me out like this, I really do.'

He scratched his chin and looked down toward the Bitterroot river, silver in the morning light.

'Tell you what. I've got a flask of lemonade in the van just crying out to be drunk. Why don't you come along and help me finish it? That way we can see if old Tansy's found her way home. What do you say?'

This time it was Eden's turn to hesitate.

'I don't know,' she said. 'We should probably be getting back.'

'Of course you should,' agreed the man. 'Only problem is, I've kind of taken you off the trail a bit. These woods can get real confusing if you don't know your way around. But there's a mountain track no more than ten minutes from here, and my van's parked at the end of it. Why don't we walk along there, have ourselves a drink and then I can drive you back to the campground?'

'Oh no, I'm sure we can find our way,' said Eden. 'We don't want to put you to any trouble.'

'It wouldn't be any trouble,' said the man. 'You've been more than kind, helping me search for my dog, and it's the least I can do.'

'OK,' said Cal, picturing ice cubes bumping around in a glass. 'That'd be great.'

He looked at Eden and could tell straight away

that she wasn't so sure. But she was the one who'd suggested a walk, the one who had wanted to trek all the way up here to look for a dog. She was the one who had made all the decisions. Now he wanted to show her that he could make a decision too.

'You coming, Eden?'

Eden nodded.

'Yeah, all right,' she said. 'I'm coming.'

NINE

The van was parked at the top of a narrow dirt track. It was a white Ford delivery van and the doors at the back had their windows painted out so you couldn't see inside. Cal noticed it was covered in a layer of dust, as if it had been there for days.

'So,' said the man, unlocking the driver's door and pulling it open. 'Who's thirsty?'

'Me,' said Eden, wiping sweat from her brow. 'Hope you've got a coupla hundred gallons stuffed away in there.'

'Oh, I've got plenty,' said the man. He reached into the glove compartment and took out a silver flask. Cal watched him unscrew the top and heard the clink of ice cubes as he poured some of the contents into it.

'Only got the one cup, I'm afraid,' he said, handing it to Eden. 'Guess we'll have to pass it around.'

He leaned against the side of the van and Cal thought it strange that he hadn't mentioned the dog.

'Still no sign of her, then?' he asked.

The man looked puzzled for a moment before seeming to remember.

'Tansy? Oh, she'll find her way back, by and by. I mean, you've got to believe that, right? You've got to believe that when you lose something you'll find it again.'

He stared at Cal with such intensity that Cal looked away.

'Because if you don't, then it just doesn't bear thinking about. I mean, what would be the point of anything, then?'

Cal saw Eden looking at him and realised she felt as uncomfortable as he did. But she tried not to let on.

'Don't worry,' she told the man. 'I'm sure he'll come back.'

'She,' said the man. 'It's *she*, goddammit!'

He glared at Eden as she passed Cal the cup and then seemed to check himself, as if realising that he had overstepped the mark.

'Hey, listen, I didn't mean to blow up at you like that,' he said. 'It's just, you know . . .' he stared at the ground as if there was something in the dirt that no one else could see. 'I just want her back. I want my Tansy to come home.'

Cal sipped the lemonade and felt it cool his throat. Beneath the chill, he thought he could taste something metallic, medicinal almost. But then this was America, where even the chocolate bars tasted weird. He took another sip and offered it to the man, who smiled and shook his head.

'No thanks,' he said. 'I've got a bottle of water to keep me going.'

Cal thought how strange it was to go to all that trouble of making yourself a flask of chilled lemonade and then not bother to drink it. But he guessed the man was just being kind and tried to remind himself that not everyone was out to get him. Maybe he just had to start believing that there were good people in this world after all.

'I'm forgetting my manners,' said the man, pushing himself away from the van and offering his hand to Eden. 'My name's Jefferson.'

Eden seemed to hesitate for a moment, then took his hand and smiled.

'I'm Eden,' she said. 'And this is Cal. I'm . . .'

She staggered forward a little and put her other hand on Jefferson's arm to steady herself. 'I don't feel so good,' she said.

Cal put down the cup and got to his feet.

'Is she OK?' he asked.

'Probably just the sun,' said Jefferson as Eden rested her head against his shoulder. 'It can do that to a person sometimes. Here, help me get her to the van.'

Cal was about to say that they had hardly been in the sun at all when Eden slumped forward and Jefferson had to use both his arms to support her.

Cal helped him take her weight and together they walked her to the back of the van. Taking the keys from his pocket, Jefferson unlocked the door and pulled it open. Inside, Cal saw that there was an old mattress and next to the mattress was a wheel brace, a shotgun and a box of cartridges.

'Hey,' he said, taking a step backwards. 'What's going on?'

But Jefferson didn't take any notice, just held Eden beneath the arms and pushed her back until she was lying on the mattress.

'What are you doing?' asked Cal. But his head hurt and the words floated away from him, up through the trees and away across the valley.

'You look tired,' Jefferson said. 'Do you want to lie down too?'

'I want to go home,' said Cal. He tried walking back towards the trees but his legs seemed full of concrete. 'Please,' he whispered. 'Take me home.'

He felt himself being dragged backwards, his heels bumping over stony ground.

Somewhere, a door slammed.

Then there was only silence.

TEN

Cal felt as though someone had lit a gallon of petrol in his brain and cracked him over the head with the empty container. He opened his eyes and found himself staring at a wooden ceiling, rough planks of pine nailed together to form a pitched roof. He was lying on a bare mattress, a thin pillow beneath his head. Gingerly rolling onto his side, he saw that the floor was also made from pine and the walls were constructed from rows of sawn timber. Although he found it hard to think straight, it was obvious that he was in some kind of log cabin.

He tried to sit up but immediately lay down again as his body gave the distinct impression that it was trying to slide up the wall, across the ceiling and back down the other side.

He moaned into the pillow and closed his eyes

again. His temples felt tender, as though something had been rubbing against his skin.

'Are you OK there, buddy?' said a voice. Cal opened one eye to see a man in check shirt and combat pants leaning against the wall in the far corner of the room. As Cal searched through the wreckage of his mind he remembered that there had been some woods, a girl, and something about a dog. The man unstuck himself from the wall and poured some water into a glass.

'Here,' he said. 'Drink this.'

Cal remembered something else then; the odd-tasting lemonade, the sky sliding away and the man opening the doors of the van.

'Get away from me!' he spat, flinging his arm out and hitting the glass so that it slipped from the man's grasp and rolled across the floor. He watched the man calmly bend down and pick it up again, the wood soaking up the spilled water as though it was as thirsty as he was.

The man set the glass back on the bedside table and poured some more water as though nothing had happened.

'You should really drink something,' he said. 'This heat'll dry a body right out.'

Cal looked at the man standing innocently by his bed like a doctor on his rounds, and remembered that his name was Jefferson. He tried to retrieve some memories from the fire that was raging in his head.

'Where's Eden?' he asked, sitting up and rubbing his temples. 'What have you done with her?'

'I haven't done anything with her. She's sleeping, is all.'

Cal glared at him. 'You put something in the drinks, didn't you?'

Jefferson shrugged.

'I needed your help.'

'So you drugged us?'

'You wouldn't have come otherwise.'

Behind the pain in his head, Cal felt a stirring of fear. A man who could drug two people just to get help was undoubtedly capable of worse. He looked around for possible escape routes and saw that the windows were single-glazed without locks. Through the one next to his bed he could see a small clearing with a bench-table in the middle, surrounded by the pale circles of a dozen tree trunks, sawn down to ground level. Cal guessed that Jefferson must have used the trees to build the cabin. Beyond the clearing, partially hidden by trees, was what appeared to be a much larger building, constructed from concrete blocks with solar panels on the roof. Apart from that there was nothing but a dense wall of trees, shadows hiding behind pine-needle skirts.

'What are you thinking?' asked Jefferson, as though everything was perfectly normal.

'I wasn't thinking anything.'

'Yes you were. You were wondering how to get away from here, weren't you?'

'Can you blame me?' said Cal. He saw no point in trying to deny it. He guessed the longer he kept the guy talking, the longer it might postpone any unpleasantness he had planned.

'I'm not going to hurt you, if that's what you're worried about. I just need your help with something, that's all. And when you've helped me, you can go.'

'What if I want to go now?'

Jefferson shrugged again.

'Well, then, I guess I can't stop you. I never lock the doors anyhow. But you should know that this place is a long way from anywhere. I decided a while back I needed a place where folks wouldn't bother me. A person walking through these woods who didn't know their way around could get pretty darn lost, in my opinion.'

Cal looked at Jefferson, standing with his arms folded, discussing the situation in such a calm, matter-of-fact manner, and his heart sank. If what he said was true, then the chances of anyone finding them were remote.

If he could just find Eden, maybe they could figure out a way of getting back to the campground before the guy took an axe to them or whatever else he had planned. But for now it was just a case of keeping him sweet while trying to survive the mother of all headaches.

'Come with me,' said Jefferson, getting up from his chair. 'There's something I want to show you.'

Eleven

Cal tried to stand and immediately sat down again, still weak from whatever it was Jefferson had put in his drink. But he didn't want to appear unwilling, so he took a deep breath and got to his feet.

'Yeah, it'll do that to you.' Jefferson nodded and smiled. 'Should wear off in an hour or so.'

He opened the door and led Cal through what appeared to be a living-cum-dining area. To one side there was a hardwood table with four chairs around it, although Cal guessed that three of the chairs probably never got used. On the table were piles of paper and a number of unwashed coffee cups, together with a jar of honey and half a loaf of bread.

In the centre of the room was a faded blue sofa with a crocheted blanket thrown over it, of the kind you might expect to see in a home belonging to an older person. There was a small kitchen at the far end, separated from the main room by a breakfast bar. On the top of the breakfast bar were more papers and a mug containing half a dozen pencils.

Jefferson liked to keep himself busy, that was for sure.

But busy doing what?

'As you can see,' said Jefferson who had noticed Cal looking around, 'I like to live a simple life. But,' he added, his eyes flashing defensively, 'don't go mistaking me for some backwoods hicky-boy with a brain in my backside. I went to college, you know.'

'OK,' said Cal, not knowing why Jefferson felt it important to tell him this.

'And not just any college, either. I was at Harvard. You know what they wrote in my high-school yearbook?'

Cal shook his head and looked at the black and white photographs on the wall of a boy with his mother, a boy with his dog. 'No. What did they write?'

'Underneath my photograph they wrote: *The boy most likely to succeed*.'

Jefferson nodded.

'And I did succeed, Cal. But that's the trouble when you're surrounded by idiots. They can't see the truth even when it's staring them in the face.'

Cal allowed himself a sideways glance at Jefferson and saw that his eyes were bright with anger. He made up his mind that, for now at least, he would do his best not to upset him. He would take his time, work out where he stood and then do everything he could to put as much distance as he could between himself and the madness that bubbled up in Jefferson's brain.

'Now it's important we all stay calm,' said Jefferson. 'I don't want anyone freaking out, right?'

'OK,' said Cal, thinking if he was going to freak out he'd have done it when he woke up to find himself stuck with a madman. But then he guessed you couldn't depend on mad people to make a whole lot of sense.

'Are you sure you're OK?' asked Jefferson as they stood outside the door of what Cal assumed was another bedroom.

'Sure,' said Cal, although he was probably further from OK than he'd been in a long while. 'Why not?'

'Good,' said Jefferson, pushing the door open.

Although the shades on the window were down, the room was dimly lit by an eerie green glow. Underneath the window on the far side of the room was a bed, and on the bed was a body covered with a white sheet. But the face was uncovered, and Cal realised that he was looking at Eden. Attached to her temples were two circular metal plates and on each plate was a small green light which stuttered and blinked. Stacked along the wall beside the bed were rows of computer towers and on the front of each one were corresponding green lights which flickered in synch with the lights on Eden's head. There was just one monitor, a single red light flickering on the side of it as if signalling some unseen exchange of information.

'I told you not to freak out, remember?' said Jefferson as Cal swore and took a couple of steps back.

'I'm not freaking out,' said Cal, fighting to remain calm.

'Then come in and close the door.'

Cal hesitated for a moment, then did as he was told. He was relieved to see the rise and fall of Eden's chest beneath the sheet, but as he wiped sweat from his palms he guessed that her well-being was not Jefferson's main concern.

'Is she OK?' he whispered, nervous of breaking the silence.

'Of course she's OK,' said Jefferson irritably, walking across to the monitor. 'She just drank more lemonade than you did, that's all.' He pushed a button on the side of the monitor and beckoned to Cal. 'Come and look.'

Cal stood beside Jefferson and stared at the screen. At first all he could see was a grey mass, colourless as a November sky. But as he watched, the mass became more defined, its edges glowing with colour. It began to dissolve and separate, forming into distinct images: a cot, a doll's house, a wooden rocking horse. Cal realised they were staring into a child's bedroom.

As they watched, the point of view changed so that Cal felt as if he was looking down at the room from somewhere up on the ceiling. He could see into the cot and there was a small child, tucked up beneath a blue blanket. On top of the blanket was a small teddy bear.

Cal heard a whimper and turned to see Eden reaching for something in her sleep.

'Well, it's nicer than her last dream,' said Jefferson. Cal waited for him to explain, but he simply nudged Cal before adding, 'OK, watch this.'

In front of the monitor was a keyboard and mouse. Cal watched as Jefferson moved the cursor across the screen. When it was on the teddy bear, he clicked the mouse and the cursor drew a box around it. The word ENLARGE? appeared on the screen with the options YES NO beneath it. Jefferson clicked YES and an image of the teddy bear filled the screen. Cal saw that the fur on the top of its head was worn smooth and that one of its eyes was missing. Jefferson clicked on it once more and this time the options CUT & SAVE and SELECT NEW OBJECT appeared. Jefferson clicked on CUT & SAVE and the image of the bedroom returned to the screen. Only this time there was no sign of the teddy bear.

In the corner of the room, Eden began to whimper once more.

'Is she OK?' asked Cal. He glanced at the monitor and saw what appeared to be dark shapes moving through the shadows of the child's bedroom.

'She's fine,' replied Jefferson, hurriedly pressing the button again so that the images shrank to a white dot and disappeared.

'Maybe I should wake her,' said Cal.

'Not yet,' said Jefferson.

Cal looked at Eden and saw that she was quieter again. Jefferson opened the door and daylight flooded into the room.

'There is something else I want to show you.'

Cal followed him through the living room and wondered whether he should make a run for it. But then he remembered what Jefferson had said about being in the middle of nowhere and guessed he was better off waiting until he could take proper stock of the situation.

Sooner or later the world would present him with another chance to move on.

Then he could run away and leave it all behind, same as he always did.

TWELVE

As they crossed the clearing, Cal felt the sun burn his neck and guessed it was probably mid-afternoon; the sky was cornflower blue and the air shimmered in the summer heat.

When they reached the concrete building, Cal was surprised at the size of it. It reminded him of the store-room at the back of the supermarket where one of his foster mums used to work. But that was stacked with enough groceries to feed a small town for a week. What possible use could Jefferson have for such a place?

Jefferson took a bunch of keys from his pocket, selected one and pushed it into the lock.

Cal remembered what he had said about never locking the doors to the house and wondered why this building should be any different.

'I built it myself,' Jefferson said, as if Cal was

a prospective buyer who had asked to be shown round. 'Took me the best part of five years.'

The door swung open and as he stepped into the corridor Cal smelled damp, stagnant air. His T-shirt stuck to his back and he shivered as Jefferson closed the door. For a moment they stood in total darkness and Cal imagined he heard whispers from somewhere at the end of the corridor. Then Jefferson flipped a switch and a neon light flickered into life. The walls were rough, unplastered breeze-block and Cal saw that there were several doors at regular intervals along the corridor, each smooth and windowless. He looked at Jefferson, his face pale beneath the artificial light, and listened to the whispers. Was this what he did for fun? Kidnapped people and kept them locked up for months, years, maybe for ever?

'What are you going to do?' he asked, trying to keep the fear out of his voice.

Jefferson saw the way Cal stared at the doors, wondering what lay behind them.

'Don't worry,' he said. 'As long as you help me, you'll come to no harm.' Then he unlocked the door in front of them, pushed it open and turned on the light.

In the centre of the room was a large metal cage.

Along the far wall was another bank of computers, their lights flickering brightly. High up in each corner were what appeared to be four satellite dishes. In the middle of each was a thin glass bulb, tapering to a point, and all four were aimed at the metal cage in the centre of the room.

'What do you think?' asked Jefferson. 'Pretty impressive, isn't it?'

Cal stayed silent, wondering whether he could move fast enough to run outside and lock Jefferson in. But Jefferson had put the keys back in his pocket and as Cal looked at his muscled arms and the rough calluses on his hands, he realised he must have spent years cutting down trees and manhandling concrete blocks in order to build this place. The work had made him strong, and Cal knew he would be no match for him in a fight.

The door of the cage was padlocked and as Jefferson unlocked it he turned to Cal and smiled.

'Works every time,' he said, pushing the door open. 'Go ahead. See for yourself.'

As Cal stood nervously at the entrance, Jefferson noticed his unease. 'What? You think I'm going to lock you in?' He turned and kicked the padlock across the floor into the corner.

'I ain't gonna lock you in.'

Cal walked into the cage and picked up the small teddy bear lying in the centre of it. Its left eye was missing and there was a worn patch on the top of its

44

head. He could see right away that it was the same as the one he had seen on the computer monitor.

'I don't understand,' he said, handing it to Jefferson. 'What do you want with me?'

'I already told you,' said Jefferson, 'I need your help.'

As he closed the door Cal thought he heard the sound again; a faint whispering, coming from the end of the corridor.

'Is there someone else here?' he asked.

Jefferson shook his head and pushed Cal out into the sunshine.

'It's just the wind in the trees,' he said, turning the key in the lock.

But the air was still; there wasn't even a breeze.

Cal sat at the table in the middle of the clearing and saw that the sun was lower in the sky now, just above the trees.

'You must be thirsty,' said Jefferson. 'You want something to drink?'

Cal nodded.

'Not lemonade,' he said.

He watched Jefferson walk back inside and wondered what he thought he was doing, bringing them out here like this. Did he really have some weird plan? Or was he just a lunatic, playing games until he grew tired of them?

And then what?

Cal didn't like to think about it. If he made a break for it now, at least he'd have a chance of escape. He tried to tell himself he hadn't known Eden that long, that it was her idea to find the dog, that it was better if at least one of them got away.

But no matter how he looked at it, he knew he couldn't leave her. He would just have to try to figure out a way of getting them both back to civilisation in one piece.

And if it meant playing along with Jefferson and whatever crazy schemes he had, then that was exactly what he would have to do.

THIRTEEN

'Here,' said Jefferson, sitting opposite him at the table. 'Two glasses of iced water.'

'Thank you,' said Cal.

Jefferson chuckled.

'What's so funny?' asked Cal.

'You English – you're so polite.'

Cal wasn't feeling very polite. He leaned over and took the glass that Jefferson had placed nearest himself.

'Don't trust me, huh?' said Jefferson, still grinning. 'Well, I can't say I blame you.'

Cal tipped his head back and drank deeply. He stared at the blue sky and wondered if he would ever see Sarah and Michael again.

'I used to be a research fellow at Harvard University,' said Jefferson. 'My subject was physics.'

He took some papers from a brown leather satchel

and pushed a black and white photograph across the table. It showed a much younger man standing on a lawn in front of a very grand looking building. He wore a suit and tie and a shirt with a button-down collar. He was fresh-faced and smiling, like a man who knew he had his whole life in front of him.

'I was twenty-three,' he said. 'Twenty-three years old and I thought nothing could touch me.'

'So what happened?' asked Cal, partly because he was interested but mainly because he wanted to keep Jefferson talking while he decided what to do.

'I was working on a new theory, working sixteen, seventeen hours a day, but I didn't care because I felt I was on the edge of something, ready to make a breakthrough. But then, two days after that photo was taken, there was a fire at my apartment. I got off the bus that night, saw the flames above my block and knew I'd lost her.'

'Lost who?'

'Tansy. My dog.'

Jefferson passed another photograph across the table.

'That's her, right there. Beautiful, isn't she?'

Cal looked at the picture of an Alsatian, sitting by a flowerbed in the middle of summer. Then he looked at Jefferson and was surprised to see that there were tears in his eyes.

'Best dog that ever lived, was Tansy. That's why I need your help, Cal. I want you to help me bring her back.' He put the photograph in his shirt pocket, next to his heart.

And at that moment, although he knew that Jefferson had done a terrible thing in bringing them here, Cal began to feel sorry for him. He knew what it was like to want something you could never have.

Still, the man was obviously deluded. If she had been in that fire, his dog was long gone. Cal decided it was safer to play along for the time being.

'But we looked for her,' he said. 'We looked all over and she wasn't there.'

'I know,' said Jefferson. He stared at Cal and tapped the side of his head. 'But that's because she's in here. And I want you to help me get her out.'

Cal shook his head.

'That's impossible,' he said.

'That's what everyone thinks. But you saw the teddy bear, right? You picked it up and held it.'

'Yeah,' Cal said slowly, 'but I don't see—'

'All right, look.'

Jefferson was animated now. He picked up a sketch pad and began to draw with quick, flowing lines.

'You see this?' He pointed to a rough drawing of a human brain. 'This is where you keep all your thoughts, your memories, all your images of the things that exist outside of your body, out in the real world. You understand?'

Cal nodded.

'OK, good. You ever watch TV?'

'Yeah, we have that in England.'

'And d'you think there are little men and women running around inside your TV set?'

'No, of course not.'

'No. But the people you see are real people, right?'

'I guess so.'

'No, you don't guess so. You *know* so. They existed in a TV studio or on a film set and then they were made into little packets of digital information. Then they were beamed into space so that they could bounce off a satellite and end up in your living room a couple of thousand miles away. Pretty incredible when you think about it, huh?'

'I suppose.'

'Trust me, it is. But go back a while. If I'd told people a hundred years ago that such a thing was possible, they'd have locked me up as a madman. It was too advanced for them and they weren't ready to believe it. Whereas nowadays we just accept it as ordinary. That old thing in the corner? It's just the TV.'

'Right,' said Cal. 'With lots of little digital people in it.' When Jefferson had started to tell him about his dog, he'd thought it might be the beginning of a normal conversation, but now he was just rambling.

'Cal!' Jefferson reached across the table and gripped his arm. 'This isn't a game. I need you to listen. It's important that you understand this.'

'I am listening,' said Cal, pulling his arm away. He had been staring into the shadows of the forest, wondering how far he would get if he ran. 'You were talking about TV.'

Jefferson reached for the sketch pad and hurriedly drew a stick figure with an arrow pointing towards the brain and another pointing back again.

'The images in your mind have their own reality, Cal, although they correspond to another reality in the physical world. But like anything else, they need energy for their existence. It was my belief that this could work both ways.'

'What do you mean?'

'I mean that if our brains can use energy to convert the reality of the physical world into an image that exists in the mind, then there had to be a way to do the opposite. To convert these images into something that exists in the physical world. Do you see?'

'Turning dreams into reality, you mean?' asked Cal.

'Exactly. Or the things in them, at any rate. No one

believed it was possible, of course. But that's because the idea is way ahead of its time. Like TV, remember? People thought it was impossible because it didn't fit with their view of the world. The world is flat, the world is round – what you believe depends on the science of the time. But then someone comes along and discovers something so incredible that people's views of the world are changed for ever.'

'And you think that's what you've done?' asked Cal, interested now in spite of his fear.

'I don't *think* I've done it, Cal. I *have* done it. And what's more, you saw me do it with your own eyes.'

Jefferson opened his satchel, took out the small brown teddy bear and placed it on the table.

'You saw this in her dreams, didn't you? You saw me take the image from her mind and turn it into something solid, something that exists out here in the real world. Don't you understand, Cal? We're making history here. This is one of those things that will change the way people see the world for ever.'

Cal looked at Jefferson and saw the way he stared at some imagined future, saw the intensity in his eyes and wondered whether the things he said could possibly be true. He knew the images on the monitor could just have been some pre-recorded piece of film, that Jefferson could have bought the bear in any one of a thousand toy shops.

But what would be the point of that? Why would Jefferson go to all the trouble of setting everything up and bringing them out here if it was simply some elaborate trick?

'Is it true?' he asked, scratching at a splinter of wood on the tabletop. 'Can you really do that?'

'Of course,' said Jefferson. 'I had to bring you out here because I needed someone young, someone with an open mind who would help me do this thing. When you've got something so huge, so important, then the normal rules don't apply. Do you see?'

Cal nodded.

'Kind of.'

And that was the strangest thing. Cal realised he was starting to believe that maybe Jefferson was telling the truth after all, that maybe all he wanted was for someone to help him with his experiment. He had a pretty extreme way of going about it, that was for sure, but then maybe if he got what he wanted, he would keep his promise.

'So now you've done it,' said Cal, 'are you going to take us back?'

Jefferson frowned.

'The thing with the teddy bear was just to prove to you that it works,' he said. 'The reason I brought you here is because I need you to do something else for me.'

'What?' asked Cal. 'What can I do?'

'Like I said,' replied Jefferson. 'I want you to find my dog. And then I want you to bring her back to me.'

FOURTEEN

'Watch carefully,' said Jefferson. 'You just press this button here, on the side of the monitor, and that gives you the picture. It's a wireless system that uses the alpha-waves the brain creates when a person is dreaming. It converts them into a different form of electrical energy which the computer system recalibrates as pixels of colour. These become the picture you see on the screen, which is an exact copy of what the person is dreaming about.'

Cal glanced across to the bed in the corner where Eden was still fast asleep. Then he turned back to the monitor which showed some kind of fairground scene and a woman whisking candyfloss onto a stick.

'That's what she's dreaming about? Candyfloss?'

'It would seem so, yes.'

Jefferson moved the mouse so that the cursor was positioned over the image of the candyfloss. 'When you find the object you're looking for, you just click on the mouse and it gives you the option to isolate it. See? You try it.'

Cal clicked on the YES option and an image of the candyfloss filled the screen. Despite the weirdness of the situation, Cal's fingers tingled with excitement.

Could he really take something from Eden's dreams and make it exist in the real world?

'All right, see now it's giving you the option to save or delete,' said Jefferson, as if he were teaching an ordinary, everyday computer class. 'When you're happy you've got the image you want, all you do is go for the save option and the computer will do the rest.'

Cal looked at the swirl of pink candyfloss on screen.

'I just click SAVE?'

'Simple as that.'

Cal clicked the mouse and heard the whirr and hum of the computers as they processed the information. He looked at the screen and saw that the candyfloss had disappeared.

'You see, Cal?'

Jefferson smiled and put a hand on his shoulder.

'Now you know what it feels like to make a dream come true.'

'Are you telling me there's now a stick of candyfloss lying in that cage?'

'Of course.'

'But how? How does it work?'

'In some ways it is very complicated, Cal. So complicated, in fact, that even the finest scientific minds have been unable to comprehend it. But in another way, it is really very simple. Just think of it like an idea.'

'An idea?'

'Yes.'

Jefferson removed the metal discs from Eden's temples and placed them beside the bed.

'Imagine that you wake up one morning and decide you want to bake a cake. You have an idea of the cake, but at this stage the cake only exists in your mind. It does not yet exist in the physical world. So you get up, and you go to the pantry, and you find all the things that you need, eggs, sugar, flour, all the ingredients that are required to bake a cake. Then put these things together in the right amounts, and you put them in the oven, and then suddenly a cake exists in the world where before there was no cake. In the morning the cake was just an idea, but in the afternoon it is a real thing that exists in the real, physical world. And so it is with dreams. All you have to do is take the energy created from the image and use it to organise the molecules in the physical world in its own likeness. The energy is the cook, and the whole world is its pantry. It contains all the ingredients it could possibly need. Do you understand?'

'Sort of,' said Cal. 'But why has no one thought of it before?'

Jefferson smiled. 'Partly because it is way more complicated than baking a cake,' he said, 'and partly because the idea is so simple. All I'm asking from you is that you help me to bring my dog back.'

'People are going to be looking for us,' said Cal. 'And when they find us, they're going to come looking for you.'

Jefferson shrugged.

'That doesn't mean they'll find me. I'm pretty good at disappearing when I have to. I've been disappearing all my life.'

The image on the monitor was flickering now, its bright colours fading to grey.

'She's waking up,' said Jefferson, walking over to the door. 'Maybe I'll just leave you two alone for a while so you can, you know, explain things to her. I wouldn't want to frighten her when she's coming around.'

Cal watched Eden moving beneath the sheets and wondered how Jefferson could possibly believe that all this was somehow going to turn out all right. But he thought that, right now, convincing Eden to play along with Jefferson's crazy scheme was probably the best chance of survival they had.

'Tell me something,' said Jefferson suddenly. 'Who is the tall tailor?'

Cal turned to see Jefferson leaning against the door frame with a strange look in his eyes, as though he was the keeper of some terrible secret.

'I— I don't know,' said Cal, but the words sent a chill through his blood, as though they had stirred something long forgotten. 'Why do you ask?'

Jefferson looked away.

'No reason,' he said. 'No reason at all.'

Then he stepped backwards and pulled the door shut, leaving Cal and Eden alone in the room.

FIFTEEN

Eden began to breathe more deeply, then gasped several times like a diver coming up for air.

'It's all right,' said Cal, standing by the bed and holding her hand. 'Everything's going to be OK.'

Eden's eyelids flickered and then she sat up and pulled her hand away.

'I'm sorry,' said Cal. 'I didn't mean—'

Eden put her hands to her face and pressed them against her eyes. Then she let them fall into her lap and stared at Cal, as if seeing him for the very first time.

'Where am I?' she asked. 'What's going on?'

'We were brought here,' said Cal. 'By the guy with the van. We were in the woods, remember?'

Eden sat on the edge of the bed, her feet dangling above the floor. She stared at her scuffed trainers as if trying to work out why she had worn them to bed.

'Right – there was a guy,' she said. 'A guy looking for his dog. He was going to drive us back.' She screwed her eyes shut and Cal remembered how much his own head had hurt when he'd woken up.

'But he drove us here instead,' he said. 'This is where he lives. Right slap-bang in the middle of nowhere.'

Eden opened her eyes again and tried to stand, but her legs were too weak and she sat down again.

'That guy brought us here?'

'Uh-huh.'

'How . . . ? Oh God, the lemonade. He spiked the lemonade, didn't he?'

Cal nodded.

'Cal, we have to get out of here.' Eden looked at the window blinds and the lights flickering on the wall of computers. She saw the metal discs on the table beside the bed and pressed a hand to her temple. 'Cal, what is going on? Is he still here?'

'He's in the living room. He wanted me to try and explain things to you.'

'What?' Eden stared at him incredulously. 'He was in here with you while I was asleep?'

'Yeah.'

'And he wants you to *explain* things? What are you, his new best friend?'

'No. I just—'

'Cal, this guy spiked our drinks and kidnapped us. For all you know he could be out there sharpening his axe, getting ready to chop us into a thousand pieces.'

'He's not like that, Eden.'

'What? Cal, are you out of your mind? We have to get out of here.'

'Yeah, well it isn't as easy as all that. Like I said, we're in the middle of nowhere.'

Eden sat up gingerly, peered through the blinds and swore.

'See?' said Cal.

'We didn't fly here by helicopter, Cal,' said Eden, lowering her voice. 'He brought us here. In a van. So if there's a way in, there has to be a way out. It stands to reason.'

'But we're miles from anywhere.'

'Says who?'

'Says Jefferson.'

'Who's Jefferson?'

'The guy.'

'Oh yeah, right. That would be the same guy who drugged us and threw us in the back of a van. No way *he'd* lie to us.'

'Look, I just think if we help him to get what he wants, he'll take us back and then this whole thing will be over with.'

'You do, huh?'

'Yes.'

'OK. And what makes you think you know what he wants?'

'Because he told me, while you were asleep.'

'I don't believe it,' said Eden, holding her head and pacing up and down. 'You're as crazy as he is.'

'Just calm down and listen for a minute,' said Cal. 'I know this must seem a bit weird to you. But just hear me out.'

'"A *bit* weird"?' Eden stood by the shutters with her hands on her hips. 'Where in England are you from – Never-Never Land? Are you going to tell me if I sit here doing nothing, my fairy godmother's gonna sweep in and take me home in a coach made out of pumpkins?'

'No,' said Cal. 'But I am going to tell you about a teddy bear you used to have.'

'What?' Eden shook her head. 'Now I know you're losing it.'

'It was brown, wasn't it? Brown with one eye missing.'

Eden looked at him and swallowed.

'How could you possibly know that?'

'Because you dreamed about it. Because I watched your dream.'

Eden looked at the computers and the monitor and the metal discs beside the bed.

'Give me a break.'

'I'm not making this up, I swear. I saw into your dreams, Eden. And it gets weirder. Jefferson says he's found a way of turning dreams into reality.'

'What?'

'He can take things from your mind and make them real.'

'Cal, I don't want to hear about it,' said Eden. 'That freak drugged me, dragged me out here and stuck things on my head. He should be locked up.'

'But if we help him . . .'

'What? No way, Cal. I ain't helping that creep. I'm gonna find him and tell him exactly what I think of him, that's what I'm gonna do. And when I've done that he's gonna drive us back home and I'm gonna make sure he spends the rest of his life eating prison food in some maximum security jail. And maybe while he's sitting there he'll think, "Oh wait a minute, maybe it wasn't such a great idea to go round kidnapping people after all."'

'I can see you're upset,' said Cal.

Eden stared at him.

'What is *wrong* with you, Cal?'

'I just think if we help him, it's our best way of getting out of here.'

'Yeah, well, that's where you and me differ,' said Eden, walking towards the door. 'You stay if you want. Me? I'm out of here.'

She pulled open the door and then hesitated. As she stepped back into the room again, Cal saw why.

Jefferson was standing in the doorway, his face white with fury.

And in his hand, he held a shotgun.

SIXTEEN

'You think it's nice to talk about people behind their backs? Do you? Huh?' Jefferson jerked the barrel of the shotgun forward as he spoke. 'Is that what you think?'

Eden raised her hands in front of her chest, as if the act of doing so might somehow stop a cartridge full of buckshot.

'I don't know what you mean,' she said, and Cal saw that her hands were trembling. 'I only just woke up. I'm still trying to figure out what's going on.'

'Oh yeah?' Jefferson kept the shotgun level as his gaze shifted from Eden to Cal and back again. 'Well, it seems like I heard you calling me a freak.'

Cal saw the flash of anger in Jefferson's eyes, saw the way his index finger curled around the trigger and decided it was time to get involved.

'She's frightened, that's all,' he said. 'She doesn't know you the way I do.'

Cal glanced at Eden and saw fear in her eyes. But he also saw the way Jefferson stared at him, like a man waking from a troublesome dream.

'You know me?' he asked, and his voice wavered. 'You *know* me?'

'I'm starting to,' said Cal. 'Just a little.'

Jefferson lowered the shotgun as if all the fight had gone out of him.

'Come out here,' he said to Eden. 'I want to prove to you that I'm not a freak.'

'How about you put the gun down first?' said Eden. 'You're making me nervous.'

'Yeah well you make *me* nervous,' said Jefferson, recovering some of his anger. 'All that talk about putting me in jail.'

'She didn't mean anything by it,' said Cal. 'She was just upset. Weren't you, Eden?'

He stared at her, willing her to play the game.

'Yeah,' she said. 'That's what it was. Now will you put the gun down?'

'All right,' said Jefferson, slowly backing out of the room. 'But don't mess with me, OK? I don't want you trying any funny stuff.'

Cal wondered what kind of funny stuff he had in

mind, but as they followed him into the living area he seemed to relax a little.

'OK, maybe I got a bit upset there,' he said, putting the gun on the table amongst the piles of papers. 'But you have to understand that I'm not out to hurt you. Look. While you were sleeping I even made you something to eat.' He went across to the breakfast bar as if nothing had happened and came back with a plate of sandwiches. Cal noticed the bread was thick and roughly cut and wondered if Jefferson had baked it himself. He imagined him standing alone in the kitchen, waiting for the dough to rise and listening to the wind in the trees.

'What's in them?' asked Eden.

'Nothing to worry about, if that's what you mean,' said Jefferson.

'I wasn't meaning that,' said Eden.

'They're cheese and tomato,' said Jefferson. 'Cheese and tomato with a touch of mayo thrown in.'

It was late afternoon and as the sun threw long shadows across the pine floorboards Cal realised how hungry he was. He thought about how he never let Sarah make breakfast for him and now here he was sitting in a log cabin taking sandwiches from a crazy man. But then Jefferson wasn't promising to look after him; he wasn't promising anything except maybe a chance to go back where he started from, and Cal was used to that.

'Not bad,' said Eden innocently, taking a bite from a sandwich. 'Where d'you get the cheese?'

'From a convenience store,' said Jefferson and Cal could tell from his face that he knew what was behind Eden's question. 'But I'd say two hours' drive ain't exactly convenient.'

'I guess not,' said Eden. She took a shifty look at the gun and Cal began to understand what Jefferson had meant about not trying any funny stuff. He tried to catch her eye, but she was too busy looking at Jefferson.

'You said you had something to show me,' she said as Cal reached for a sandwich and perched on the arm of the sofa. 'Something to prove you're not a freak, remember?'

Cal could see she was still angry, that she was deliberately pushing Jefferson, trying to goad him into an anger that would match her own. But Jefferson didn't seem to notice. Instead he simply said, 'That's right,' and disappeared into the bedroom. When he returned, Cal saw that he was holding something behind his back.

'Shut your eyes,' he said, grinning like it was some kind of birthday surprise. 'Shut your eyes and hold out your hands.'

Eden glanced at Cal and he nodded, so she did as Jefferson had asked. When her eyes were closed, Jefferson produced the teddy bear from behind his back and placed it in her hands with a flourish.

'There,' he said proudly. 'What do you think of that?'

Eden opened her eyes and stared at the teddy bear.

'What's this?' she asked.

'I should have thought that was obvious,' said Jefferson. 'It's a teddy bear. Or rather, I should say, it's *your* teddy bear.'

Eden turned it over in her hands and Cal watched as her fingers stroked the worn patch of fur, touching the frayed threads where the glass eye used to be.

'Where did you get this?' she whispered.

Jefferson smiled.

'From inside your head,' he said.

SEVENTEEN

'Do you think I'm stupid?' There was a hard edge to Eden's voice now, like water turning to ice. 'This whole thing you told Cal about turning dreams into reality. You might have talked him into believing it, but if you think you're going to get me to go along with it then you're even crazier than you look. And that's saying something.'

Jefferson clenched his jaw so tight that Cal could see the tendons in his neck.

'So how do you explain this?' he asked, snatching the teddy bear from her hand and shaking it angrily. 'How do you explain it? Hmm?' He was shouting now but it felt like only the beginning, the first gasping breaths of a toddler before the tantrum.

'How do I explain it?' replied Eden. 'Well, let's see. Maybe the kind of guy who's willing to hang around a campground and drug people is also the kind of

71

guy who is going to wait around outside a person's house and steal their stuff.' She glared at Jefferson. 'That's it, isn't it? You broke into my house and took it, just so you could live out your weird fantasy about making dreams come true. Well, I've got news for you, buddy. I don't believe a word of it. Like I said before, you're crazy. A crazy freak.'

'What did you say?'

'You heard me.'

Jefferson dropped the teddy bear and clenched his fists.

'You think I'm crazy?' he said. 'Well maybe I'll just show you some of the other things I found in that twisted brain of yours. Then we'll see who the crazy one really is.'

Cal was still trying to work out what he meant when Eden leapt across the room, grabbed the shotgun from the table and pointed it at Jefferson's head.

'All right,' she said. 'Give me the keys to the van.'

Cal looked at her incredulously.

'Eden, what are you doing? You can't even drive.'

'Oh yeah? Just watch me.'

'Don't be a fool,' said Jefferson, holding out his hand. 'Give it to me.'

'Oh, I'll give it to you all right,' said Eden, holding the shotgun level and backing towards the door. 'Come any closer and I'll give you both barrels.'

Jefferson didn't seem to hear her. Or if he did, he didn't take any notice. Tight-lipped with anger, he strode across the floor and closed his hand around the end of the gun.

'Now what are you going to do?' he asked. 'Are you going to kill me? Or are you going to stop this nonsense so that everyone can go home?'

Cal saw the hesitation in Eden's eyes and knew that Jefferson saw it too. When he pulled on the end of the gun, there was no resistance; Eden loosened her grip and he took the weapon and placed it on the table.

'You don't have to hate me, you know,' he said.

Eden narrowed her eyes, concentrating all her emotions into a single stare.

'I don't have to like you either,' she said.

Jefferson's lip quivered momentarily and it made Cal think of a small boy standing alone in a play-ground, waiting to join in the others' games.

But then Jefferson's anger returned.

'We can do this easy,' he said, 'or we can do it hard. Either way, it's going to get done. So what do you say?'

'I say we do it easy,' said Cal quickly, before Eden could start another argument. 'Why don't you go and lie down, get yourself comfortable? Then when you're ready, we'll see about finding your dog.'

'Is that a promise?' asked Jefferson suspiciously. 'Do you give me your word?'

Cal nodded.

'I promise,' he said.

When he heard this, Jefferson seemed to calm down a little. He walked across to the kitchen cupboard and took out a mug and a bottle of whisky.

'I don't want your friend in there,' he said, half-filling the mug with whisky and taking a mouthful. 'She'll ruin it. Same as she probably ruins everything. I knew I shoulda left her back there in the woods.'

'Whatever you want, OK?' said Cal as Eden sat on the sofa and folded her arms, refusing to look at them. 'Whatever you want.'

Outside, the sun was setting and a pale moon rose above the trees.

Jefferson lit the oil lamp and placed it on the table. Then he walked towards the bedroom with the whisky in one hand and the mug in the other. He stopped in the doorway and turned back to look at Eden. 'You upset me, you know that? How am I going to find my dog with all that bad energy running around in my head?'

'Maybe you should have thought of that before you drugged me and threw me in your van,' said Eden.

Jefferson took a slug of whisky straight from the bottle and shook his head.

'Just keep her away from me, OK?' he said. Then he walked into the bedroom and closed the door.

'What are you doing?' hissed Cal.

Eden turned to look at him, her green eyes sparkling with anger.

'What am I doing? What are *you* doing, more like.'

'I'm trying to get us out of here without anyone getting killed.' He looked at the gun on the table. 'And I mean *any*one.'

'I should have done it,' said Eden. 'I should have pulled the damn trigger.'

'Yeah, because you so would,' said Cal.

'How do you know I wouldn't?'

'Because you're a good person,' Cal replied. 'And good people don't kill other people.'

'Maybe they do if they have to.' Eden walked over to the table and picked up the shotgun.

'Don't, I mean it,' warned Cal. 'Let's just do what we have to do and get out of here.'

'My thoughts exactly,' said Eden. She turned the shotgun over in her hands and Cal guessed she must have handled one before on her dad's farm. Holding the barrels in one hand and the stock in the other, she put it over her knee and broke it open.

'Well I'll be,' she said.

She turned the gun around to show Cal.

'It was never loaded,' she said. 'The chambers are empty.'

'That's what I was trying to tell you. He doesn't want to hurt us, Eden. He just wants us to help him. And when we've done that, we can go home.'

'You really believe that, don't you?'

'Yeah. What's wrong with that?'

'You're a fool, Cal. Don't you see? There's no way he's going to let us go after this. He knows if he does then the authorities are going to find him and lock him up for a long, long time. You really think he's going to let that happen?'

Cal shrugged.

'Maybe we don't have to tell anyone.'

'What? And let that freak do the same thing to some other poor kids? I don't think so.'

'He gave me his word,' said Cal. 'And I gave him mine.'

'Yeah, well you'll excuse me if I don't share your faith in human nature.'

Eden glanced at the door and then lowered her voice.

'While he's busy drinking himself to sleep in there, I'm going to get busy finding the keys to his van. And when I do, I'm out of here. Now are you with me, or are you going to stay here and play let's pretend?

Cos I'm telling you, Cal, when he finally realises this whole thing is just a product of his warped imagination, he's going to flip.'

'I don't think so. I don't think he's like that.'

'You've got to stop kidding yourself, Cal. You saw how crazy he got when he heard me talking about him.'

'That's because you called him a freak. And he isn't a freak. He's just trying to get back something he lost.'

'OK, Cal, you know what? I can't deal with this. Either you come with me now, or I'm going to have to go without you.'

Cal shrugged.

'You do what you want. But I think you're making a big mistake.'

'No, Cal, you're the one making the mistake.' As Cal turned towards the bedroom, she tried one last time.

'Please, Cal. Don't do it. Come with me.'

'I can't,' said Cal. 'Like I said. I gave him my word.'

Then he went into the room and closed the door behind him.

EIGHTEEN

The room was dark, lit only by the faint glow from the computer screen. Jefferson was lying on his side, clutching the empty whisky bottle to his chest. When he saw Cal, he leaned over and placed the bottle on the floor.

'I'm ready,' he said. He looked past Cal towards the open door. 'Where's your friend? Planning new ways to mess things up?'

Cal shook his head.

'She doesn't want to get involved.'

'Good,' said Jefferson, fastening the metal discs to the side of his head.

'You remember what to do?'

'I think so,' said Cal. He stood beside the monitor and watched a snowstorm of static fizz across the screen. 'I'm not getting any pictures.'

'That's because it's not tuned into conscious

thought,' said Jefferson, settling back onto the pillow. 'Nothing will happen until I reach the second phase of sleep. That's when you'll start getting images. And when you see my dog, I want you to move in and grab her.'

'With the cursor?'

'Same as I showed you before. Isolate her, cut her out and the machine will do the rest.'

'You might not even dream about her, though.'

'Believe me, I will. She's all I ever dream about.'

From his top pocket Jefferson took out the photograph he'd shown Cal earlier and held it between the tips of his fingers.

'Take it. Remind yourself what she looks like.'

Cal took the photograph and studied it closely.

'She was a nice-looking dog,' he said.

Jefferson nodded.

'Best friend I ever had.'

Cal stared at the walls of the cabin that Jefferson had built miles from anywhere and wondered if she was the only friend he ever had.

'I'll hang on to this, shall I?' he asked. 'Just to make sure.'

'Yeah. You do that.'

As Jefferson sank deeper into his pillow, Cal put the photograph next to the monitor and wondered if Eden had found the van keys. If she had, he hoped

Jefferson wouldn't hear her start the engine. He was determined to do this now, determined to help Jefferson find what he was searching for, no matter what Eden or anyone else might think. Naturally, he was curious, but more than that, it felt like he would be doing a good thing, and Cal couldn't remember the last time he had felt that way about anything.

'You're a good kid,' Jefferson murmured as he closed his eyes. 'You know that, don't you?'

The monitor was flickering, reds and greens bleeding from the edges and mixing together in the centre of the screen. Cal looked up and saw that Jefferson's hands were folded across his chest, like a knight lying in state. His breathing was deeper now, eyelids twitching as his eyes followed the dreams that emerged from the shadows of his mind.

The colours on the screen were starting to blend, solidifying into the reds and browns of autumn leaves. As they floated from the trees, adding to those already carpeting the forest floor, Cal saw, through a gap in the branches, a path leading down to a lake. He glanced across at Jefferson, astonished to think that he was witnessing the scene unfolding inside his head. Turning his attention back to the screen, he saw that something was waiting by the water's edge. The picture began moving rapidly towards it, as if the person in the dream had started to run.

The colours were glowing, so sharp and bright that Cal felt almost as if he was having the dream himself. His heart beat faster as he realised that the image beside the lake was that of a dog.

Tansy.

As the image came closer, Cal used the mouse to position the cursor in the centre of it. He was about to click on the mouse when he noticed something moving in the left of the picture.

It was a red-haired girl, waving her arms about and shouting, and as Cal realised that the girl looked very much like Eden, the dog bared its teeth and snarled. Then Cal clicked the mouse and the image froze, captured in mid-snarl by a red outline. The word ENLARGE? appeared on the screen and Cal clicked the YES option, then CUT & SAVE and the image of the lake returned to the screen. Only this time there was no sign of the dog.

In the corner of the room, Jefferson began to whimper softly.

'Cal,' hissed a voice behind him. 'Cal!'

Cal turned to see Eden standing in the doorway, silhouetted in the light from the living room.

'What are you doing here?' he asked. 'I thought you'd gone.'

Eden held up a set of keys and dangled them from side to side. 'I found these in the kitchen drawer.

They don't open the van, but maybe there's another one somewhere. Want to help me look?'

Cal saw that they were the keys Jefferson had used to open the door of the building across the clearing.

'I know what they're for,' he said, switching off the monitor. Jefferson turned to face the wall, but Cal could see from the slow rise and fall of his shoulders that he was still asleep. 'Come on.'

'Wait,' said Eden, 'I'm taking the gun.'

'It's not loaded, remember?'

'Doesn't mean he can't load it when he wakes up.' Eden picked the shotgun up off the table and followed Cal across the living room to the back door.

'Where are we going?'

'I need to check on something,' said Cal. 'I need to make sure I did it right.'

He stepped outside and smelled the heavy fragrance of pine needles in the warm night air. The trees were silhouetted against a sky full of stars.

'It'll only take a minute. If everything's OK, I'll have kept my side of the bargain and Jefferson will have to take us home.'

'You really believe in this whole dream thing, don't you?'

'Yeah. I guess I do.'

Eden rested the shotgun barrels in the dirt and

stared at him. 'OK. But if it hasn't worked, will you come with me?'

'It will work, Eden. I've seen it.'

'But if it doesn't?'

Cal remembered Jefferson's anger when Eden had called him crazy. He thought of the image of her in his dream and the vicious snarl of the dog.

'If it doesn't, then I'll come,' he said.

Nineteen

When they reached the building, Cal sorted through the keys until he found the one Jefferson had used to open the door. The metal was rusted, small flakes of silver lifting along the length of the stem.

As Cal turned the key, Eden put a hand on his arm.

'Listen,' she said.

Cal heard a whisper like the wind in the trees.

'It's nothing,' he said. 'It's only the wind.'

But as he stepped into the corridor the sound became more insistent and for a moment he thought he heard someone speak his name. Then the sound stopped and he turned to see Eden waiting at the doorway, still listening.

'It came from down there,' she said. 'I'm sure of it.'

'Can you hear it now?'

Eden stepped into the corridor and shook her head.

'No,' she said. 'I don't hear anything now.'

They walked down the corridor a little way until they came to the first room, the room where Jefferson had shown Cal the teddy bear.

'OK, this is the place,' said Cal, searching for the key.

'What place?'

'The place where the objects materialise.'

'Oh yeah, right. Of course.'

Eden glanced back the way they had come as if she had already decided that this was going to be a waste of time. But as Cal pushed the door open and fumbled for the light switch, he heard the unmistakable sound of a dog growling.

As the bare thirty-watt bulb glowed dull orange he saw the dog crouching in the middle of the cage with its hackles raised.

'Hey there, Tansy,' he said. 'Good dog. Everything's going to be all right.'

But as he approached the cage, the dog's ears flattened against its head and it launched itself at the bars, barking and snapping its jaws together.

Cal jumped backwards and Eden pulled him out into the corridor, slamming the door shut.

'What have I done?' he whispered.

'I don't know,' said Eden, clearly shocked by what she had just seen. 'What *have* you done?'

'I think I got it too early,' said Cal. 'I clicked on it when it was mad at you or something, and now it just seems crazy.'

'What do you mean, mad at me?' asked Eden. 'I've never seen it before in my life.'

'I know, but you were there in Jefferson's dream. I saw you. Maybe it's because you had that argument or something. But you came and scared the dog and now I'm worried it's not the dog he was hoping for.'

'Is all this really true?' asked Eden, running her hand through her hair. 'With the dog and my teddy bear and everything?'

'Take a look in there if you don't believe me,' said Cal. 'There's nothing made up about that dog, I can tell you.'

Eden leaned against the door frame and although she was in shadow, there was enough moonlight for Cal to see that she was afraid.

'This is crazy,' she said. 'Insane.'

'I know,' said Cal. 'I tried to tell you.'

Although the door was closed, Cal could hear the muffled barks and the clanking of the cage as the dog continued to throw itself against the bars.

'We have to go before Jefferson wakes up,' said

Eden. 'When he finds out what's happened to his dog, he'll go nuts.'

'But how? You said you couldn't find the keys.'

'Maybe he's got them in his pocket or something. How was he when you left him?'

Cal shrugged. 'He was pretty much out of it.' He looked at Eden doubtfully. 'Since when have you been able to drive?'

'Dad lets me drive his truck around the farm sometimes.'

'Have you ever driven on the road?'

'No, but how hard can it be? You turn the wheel when you want to go round corners and hit the brakes when you don't. It's no big deal.'

'So you're saying we just take his keys and drive out of here?'

'Yes, Cal. That's exactly what I'm saying.'

'But what about Jefferson?'

'What about him?'

'He'll be left miles from anywhere without any transport.'

'Yeah, well you can worry about that if you want to. I'm more worried about what he's gonna do when he wakes up and finds out you've turned his favourite dog into a psycho. Now are we going to do this, or what?'

Cal leaned his head back against the wall and sighed.

'OK, let's do it.'

He was about to step out through the door when he heard the whispering again. It was louder now, more insistent. And then came the words, soft but unmistakable:

Help me.

Let me out.

'Cal,' said Eden, her voice trembling. 'I think there's someone down there.'

TWENTY

As they crept down the corridor they passed two locked doors and Cal began to wonder if he had been wrong about Jefferson. Were there others who had believed his promises, only to find themselves locked away? The faint light from the entrance to the building was some way behind them now and as they reached the end of the corridor it was almost impossible to see.

'Are you still there?' whispered Eden as he slid his shoulder along the wall, feeling for a doorway.

'I'm here,' he said, touching her arm for reassurance.

'There's another door here,' whispered Eden. He heard the rattle of metal as she tried the handle. 'I think it's locked.'

Cal pressed his ear against the cold steel and listened.

I know you're out there, whispered a voice. *I can hear you breathing.*

As Cal stepped back in alarm, Eden brushed past him and put her own ear against the door.

'It sounds like a child,' she said. 'It's saying it wants to be let out because it's frightened of the dark.'

Cal immediately felt his fear replaced by anger; anger that Jefferson had lied to him, that he could take a child and lock them away in the name of scientific research.

'Don't worry,' he called, reaching into his pocket and pulling out the keys. 'We're coming.'

As he tried first one key and then another, the voice became more urgent, whispering, *Hurry, hurry, you must let me out*, and as he finally found the right key and fitted it into the lock, the voice whispered, *I have been waiting so long for you, Cal*, and Cal thought how strange it was that the child should know his name.

Then the door swung open and he saw that the voice didn't belong to a child at all, but to a tall man standing in the shadows. His white, smiling face seemed all too familiar and Cal immediately recognised the top hat, the green frock coat and the shiny black shoes from the drawings in his notebook.

'Hello, Cal,' whispered the man. 'Remember me?'

Then he stepped out of the shadows and held up a pair of long silver scissors.

'I hope you're not going to scream,' he said. 'But I think you probably will.'

Cal felt the shadows swirl and then Eden shouted, pulling him backwards and slamming the door shut. He heard footsteps across the floor and Eden screamed at him to run but he had seen the size of the man and knew he could never outrun him. And so, as their footsteps echoed down the corridor, he found himself standing in the first room, fumbling with the lock. Then the cage door was open and the dog was out, snarling past him and hurling itself into the corridor. And suddenly Cal was out beneath the stars with Eden beside him and they were running through the trees and into the forest. And all he could think of was that he should have listened, should have listened to her in the first place, but now it was too late and the darkness had found him and now they were going to die.

Branches cracked underfoot.

An owl rose from the trees, hooting out a warning before flapping away into the night. Cal heard the gasp of Eden's breath and the thump of her footsteps as they pushed deeper into the forest, desperate to get away.

'Cal!'

For a moment Cal thought that the man had caught up with them, but as he spun round he saw that Eden had tripped over a tree root and was sprawled across a layer of pine needles, the shotgun lying on the ground next to her.

'Cal, help me!' she cried, and Cal was afraid, knowing that the man could not be far behind. Grabbing her beneath the arms, he pulled her roughly to her feet, dragging her against a tree before pressing himself against the bark and turning his head to see if there was any sign of the man. But all he saw was the outline of the pines, and the dark shadows beneath their branches.

'We can't stay here,' he whispered, trying to keep the fear from his voice. 'We have to keep going.'

Eden bent down and massaged her ankle.

'How is it?'

'It's fine. It's just a knock.'

Cal saw how she winced when she put her weight on it, but he wasn't about to argue.

'All right,' he said. 'Let's go.'

Eden slid the empty shotgun beneath a fallen tree and they stumbled blindly onwards, not caring what lay ahead, only wanting to put as much distance as they could between themselves and the man with the pale, bloodless smile. Cal felt the pine needles scratching his skin and as they went deeper into the forest the trees thickened until the glow from the stars faded and there was no light at all.

'Cal, wait!'

'I'm over here!' Cal answered, listening to her moving through the undergrowth. 'I'm here,' he said again, more quietly now, scared that someone might hear. And then, in the darkness, he sought out Eden's hand, because he was afraid of being alone.

'Do you think we lost him?' Eden whispered, so close that he could feel her heart beating.

'I don't know,' said Cal. 'I think we should keep going for a while.'

'Who was he?' breathed Eden.

'I don't know,' said Cal. 'Although I recognise him from somewhere. I think I've dreamed about him. And I kind of . . . drew pictures of him.'

'You did *what*?'

'I know. I'm still trying to get my head round it. But I think Jefferson may have taken him from my dreams. He's dangerous, Eden, That's why we have to keep moving.'

'OK,' said Eden. 'But I think we should go back and check on the dog.'

'What?'

'It wasn't angry at me at all. It went for the guy when he came out of his cell. It saved us, Cal. I just

93

want to know it's all right. It was yelping like mad when we left.'

Cal shook his head, amazed that she could be thinking of the dog at a time like this.

'There is no *way* we're going back there now, Eden. The dog will be fine. That guy is crazy, OK? He wants to kill us. We have to get out of here.'

As they went deeper into the forest, the darkness thickened around them. Whenever a dry branch cracked underfoot they stopped, frozen with fear, listening for signs that someone was following them. Cal slowed down until he could feel Eden's breath on the back of his neck, then advanced step by careful step, his hands held out to protect himself from whatever might be lurking in the blackness.

After a while he found that his senses were so heightened by fear and the lack of vision that – between the scratch of branches and the rough bark of the trees – he became aware of something else; of blood pulsing beneath his skin and the warm night air moving above it. And because he could no longer see where he ended and the world began, he started to feel that somehow the world itself was aware of him. As if even the air knew that there was only this thin layer of skin separating him from the rest of the world and everything in it.

'Cal! *Cal!*'

Eden's urgent whispers broke into his thoughts.

'What is it?'

'I hear something.'

Cal stopped and listened.

At first all he heard was the wind in the trees. But then he heard the rush and whisper of something else and realised that it was the sound of water.

'Come on,' he said.

As they got closer, the trees thinned out and the darkness lightened until they saw the shapes of branches and roots and the glitter of stars overhead.

'Look,' said Eden, 'over there.'

She pointed through the trees and Cal saw a mountain stream, flowing over rocks and stones towards the valley.

Although Cal was still afraid, there was something about the sight of running water that lifted his spirits.

'It's beautiful,' said Eden, and for a few moments they stood beside it in silence.

Then Eden turned to Cal and nudged him.

'You know what we should do?'

'No. What?'

'We should build a shelter.'

'What for?'

'Because that's what you do when you get stuck in the woods. It keeps you warm and dry.'

'I'm already warm and dry. And anyway, we should keep going. The guy, remember?'

'Cal, there's no way he'll find us now. We had a head start on him and we've been all over since then. Even *we* don't know where we are.'

'I know, but—'

'I just think we're better off trying to find a way out of here in the morning when it's light. And a shelter's better than sleeping out in the open.'

Cal stared at her.

'You really want to build this shelter, don't you?'

'I really do.'

'Were you in the Girl Guides or something?'

'Girl Scouts. Troop leader.'

In spite of himself, Cal smiled.

'You don't say.'

He looked around.

'So what do we have to do, exactly?'

Eden smiled back.

'Watch and learn,' she said.

TWENTY-ONE

Cal was amazed at how skilful Eden was, considering that the only tools she had were her hands. First she searched around until she found a fallen branch, stripping off the side growth until she had a piece of wood the thickness of her forearm. Pushing one end through the layer of pine needles into the soil below, she wedged the other end against a tree trunk to form a triangle. Then, with Cal's help, she broke off some of the lower branches from the surrounding trees and leaned them, fan-like, against the central branch. Finally she laid more branches horizontally across before weaving them all together.

'There,' she said when they had finished. 'What do you think?'

'Not bad,' said Cal. 'What do you do for an encore?'

'I go inside and lie down,' said Eden. 'Coming?'

Cal followed her inside, breathing the sweet smell of pine sap as he covered the entrance with branches and lay down beside her.

'This doesn't feel real,' she whispered. 'I feel as if I'm going to wake up any minute and my mom will be standing there, asking me what I want for breakfast.'

'Do you wish you were back there?' asked Cal. 'Back at the camp, I mean.'

'Of course. Don't you?'

'Kind of. To tell you the truth, none of my life seems real anyway.'

'What do you mean?'

Cal thought for a moment, trying to find the right words.

'Sometimes my life just feels like something I don't have any say in. People telling me, *Do this*, *Do that*. It's like I'm watching myself in a film, where all the lines are already written. But out here, I'm away from all that. There's no one organising my life or telling me what to do. I just . . . am.'

Eden propped herself up on her elbow and turned to face him.

'Cal? You remember when we were walking up the trail before?'

'Yeah. What about it?'

'You told me they weren't your real parents. And then you just kind of clammed up.'

'That's because it's not very interesting.'

'*I'm* interested.'

'OK. I'm what they call a child looked after. What they used to call a foster kid. Which basically means I get to stay with a new family for a while until they decide they've had enough of me. Then I get sent back to the residential centre until they find someone else.'

'Huh.'

Cal could almost hear the click of Eden's brain cells as she tried to make sense of it. 'So why can't you just stay with one family?'

'Because I don't want to. What's the point? I know it's not going to last.'

'How?'

'Because I've been there before. Foster parents are there to look after you until you get a family that wants to adopt you, that's all. And I was going to be adopted by this family one time, and I was all set to go with my suitcase packed and everything, and then the social worker comes in and sits me down and says, basically, it's not going to happen.'

'Why not?'

'I don't know. They split up or something. And after that, I thought, you know, what's the point?

You get all ready, thinking someone's going to come along and make your life better. And it's not true. No one's going to do that. Ever.'

'Someone might,' said Eden.

'No,' said Cal, 'they won't. Which is why I don't bother getting to know them any more. And it's why I like being out here, away from all that stuff. It's too complicated.'

'What about me?' said Eden.

Cal was puzzled.

'What about you?'

'You're getting to know me, aren't you?'

'That's different.'

'How is it different?'

'Because you don't expect anything of me, that's why. You know that when all this is over, we're going to go our separate ways.'

'Like life, you mean.'

'What?'

'When it's over, we go our separate ways.'

Cal frowned.

'Are you making fun of me?'

'No. I'm saying that just because something's going to end doesn't mean it shouldn't begin.'

Cal shook his head.

'You've lost me,' he said.

'I think maybe you've lost yourself,' said Eden.

'Maybe that's why you like it out here where no one can see you.'

'You can see me.'

'I'm starting to. But there's a ways to go yet.'

Eden laid her head on her hands and closed her eyes.

'I hope you get some sleep.'

'Maybe we'll find our way out of the woods to-morrow,' said Cal.

'Maybe we will.'

When she was asleep, Cal lay on his back and stared at the ridge of branches above him. If he moved his head slightly, he could see the sky through a tiny gap. And in the middle of that vast darkness was a single star, its light scattered through time and space until the last shining remnants fell through the forest into the lens of his eye.

He remembered watching a TV programme which said that the light from a star takes so long to reach the earth that by the time you see it, the star might no longer exist.

He looked at Eden lying next to him with her eyes closed and thought how quiet it was when she was asleep.

Just because something's going to end, doesn't mean it shouldn't begin.

He didn't know what made her come up with stuff like that.

But what he did know, lying there in the darkness and looking up at a solitary star, was that his heart ached and there wasn't a thing in the world he could do about it.

TWENTY-TWO

Cal awoke to a curious metallic sound; precise and surgical. He glanced at Eden, but she had turned away from him and the only noise she made was the soft ebb and flow of her breathing. Fingers of moonlight slid through the branches above his head.

He heard the noise again.

Anxious not to make a sound, Cal sat up until his head was almost touching the branches at the top of the shelter.

Something was definitely out there.

Cal shivered. If he woke Eden, the noise would almost certainly give them away. But if he moved quietly enough, maybe he could slip out without being seen and discover what was out there. Quite what he would do if he found out, he didn't know, but at least he would know what he was dealing with.

On his hands and knees now, Cal carefully removed the covering of branches at the entrance of the shelter and crawled outside. The temperature had dropped beneath a clear sky and the moon had risen above the trees, bathing the forest in a pale white light.

The trees were stark and unfamiliar in the moonlight, formless shadows lurking beneath their branches. Careful to avoid stepping on any twigs which might betray his location, Cal moved soundlessly away from the shelter and positioned himself behind the trunk of a tree.

Pressing his cheek against the rough bark, he listened.

In the distance, he heard the rush and chatter of the stream.

A mosquito whined in his ear.

Then the sound again.

Snip, snip, snip.

It was fainter now, further away, mixing with the sound of the water.

Realising he had been holding his breath, Cal allowed himself to breathe again, running his tongue over dry lips.

He moved quickly to the cover of the next tree, then the next, listening each time for the clipped, metallic sound to start again. But he could no longer hear it. The sound had stopped.

As he approached the stream, he hid himself behind another tree and listened intently. But all he could hear was a soft breeze stirring the branches and the sound of water tumbling over stones.

The sky was lightening in the east and the stars were already fading; it would soon be morning. Cal realised how tired he was and remembered how once, when he was small, he had imagined his room to be full of ghosts. He had watched in terror as the dark shapes crept across his bedroom wall until it had occurred to him that it was only the shadow of the curtains, moving in the evening breeze.

That's all this is, he told himself. *I'm jumping at shadows*. Feeling a little foolish, he decided he would get a drink from the stream and then head back to the shelter. With any luck he would get back before Eden woke up and realised he was gone.

Stepping out of the shadows, he knelt on the mossy ground beside the stream and splashed his face several times before quenching his thirst from the leaking cup of his hands. The cool water soothed him but as he wiped his mouth and raised his head he saw – some way off – someone standing in the stream. His first reaction was to run, but then he realised that whoever it was had their back to him, so he stepped back behind the tree again before peering around for a better look.

He could tell from the figure's height and stance that it was a man, although his hair was long and brushed the tops of his shoulders as he leaned forward into the stream. As the sky grew lighter, Cal saw that the man's hair was dark brown, almost red, the colour of clay or dried blood and he wore an old-fashioned frock coat, but not the traditional black one might expect; this one was the green of algae in a stagnant pond. On his bottom half he wore a pair of breeches which stopped at the knee, covering a pair of long white socks that disappeared beneath them. As the first rays of sunlight rimmed the distant mountains with gold, Cal could see the man's white socks beneath the surface of the stream and below them a pair of black, pointed shoes with polished silver buckles.

His coat tails dipped in the water and he moved slowly from side to side, as if he was washing something in the stream.

Cal looked at the black top hat placed neatly on the far bank and knew, with an awful, sickening certainty, that it was the man from his drawings, the same man he had caught sight of in the shadows of the cell, and that the noise he had heard had been the *snip, snip, snip* of metal on metal.

But what did he want with Cal?

As the sun rose over the mountains, Cal saw dark ribbons twisting through the water and realised that the stream was red with blood. Then the man turned and lifted the scissors he was holding. But they were no ordinary scissors. These were more like shears with long, polished blades as sharp as daggers.

As the man turned and stared at him, Cal guessed he had sensed him watching all along. Without dropping his gaze, the man raised his arms until the scissors were pointing straight at Cal.

He nodded slowly, three times, as if to say, *Yes, it will happen, never doubt or question it.*

Then Cal was running through the woods, desperate to be anywhere but in this place where the man with the scissors was waiting to drag him down, away from the light for ever.

TWENTY-THREE

'Take it easy, Cal,' said Eden, shaking him roughly by the shoulders. 'Just tell me what happened.'

Cal crouched beside the shelter, staring back through the trees.

'Cal! Speak to me!'

'He's here,' said Cal.

'Who? Who's here?'

'He had shears, silver ones. He was washing blood from them in the stream.'

'Look at me, Cal,' said Eden, holding his face in both her hands. 'Who was washing them?'

'Him,' said Cal. 'The man from the cell.'

'Are you sure? It was pretty dark back there.'

'Yeah, it was him all right. He wore old-fashioned clothes. Like someone from a storybook. And he just kept staring at me and all the blood was in the river and then he pointed at me with those shears. He wants to kill me, Eden. I know he does.'

Eden took her hands from his face and rested them on his shoulders.

'No one's going to kill you, Cal. Not if I've got anything to do with it.'

She looked at the rays of morning sunlight filtering through the trees.

'Do you think he followed you?'

'I don't know. Maybe. I was too busy running.'

'You don't think he was just some ordinary guy? Like a hunter, cleaning his knife in the stream, and you got freaked out because you weren't expecting it?'

Cal shook his head.

'I know what I saw, Eden. And he's out there. He's out there looking for me. For us.'

'All right, listen,' said Eden. 'Maybe you should tell me about those pictures.'

'What pictures?'

'You said you'd done some drawings of him.'

Cal looked over his shoulder, afraid that the man might already have tracked him down.

'When we were travelling in the camper van,' he said, lowering his voice, 'I kept having these nightmares. And I kept doing this same drawing of a man in a long green coat with a top hat, carrying scissors all covered in blood. And that's the man I saw just now. Down by the stream.'

At this, Eden seemed to relax a little.

'Cal, how much sleep did you get last night?'

'Why?'

'I'm just asking.'

'Oh no.' Cal got up and shook his head. 'You think I'm making this up, don't you?'

'No, I don't think that. I just think sometimes when you haven't had much sleep, your mind plays tricks on you. And you said yourself, this guy looked exactly like some drawing you'd done.'

'I know, but—'

'You're exhausted, Cal. We both are. But think about it for a moment. How likely is it that you're going to go walking through a forest in the middle of Montana and find some guy dressed up like a character from a storybook?'

'But it's the guy from the cell. I know it is.'

'It was dark, Cal. And we've both been drugged, remember? Stuff like that can really mess with your mind.'

'All right, then,' said Cal, 'think about this. You go for a walk in the forest and a guy drugs you and puts you in a van. You wake up and you find yourself wired up to a machine and the guy says he's just doing it because he wants his dog back. He shows you an old teddy bear which you've had ever since you were a kid, complete with missing eye and he tells you that he fished it out of your dreams. How am I doing so far?'

Eden shrugged, but didn't say anything.

'Then you pick up the guy's shotgun and threaten him with it. You have an argument and then agree to wire him up to his machine so you can use it to get his dog back for him. But because of the argument he's angry, which affects his brain and means that the dog comes out crazy. Then you go to a concrete building in the middle of nowhere and the dog's there, and you hear whispering and then you see a crazy guy in the shadows and you make a run for it. Did you imagine all that too? Or do you actually believe that some of it might be real?'

Eden leaned back against a tree and sighed.

'I'll tell you what I do believe,' she said. 'I believe that right now, I don't know anything about anything. Except that you and me have to find a way of getting out of here and finding our way back home. And as far as I'm concerned, I'll do whatever it takes to get there.'

Cal looked up through the trees at the sun as it climbed into a clear blue sky. He listened to the birdsong and the insects chirping in the heat.

'OK,' he said. 'Whatever it takes.'

Then they turned and walked deeper into the shadows of the forest.

Twenty-Four

Jefferson woke to the hum of computers and the striped shadows of the window blind falling across his sheet. Pulling the discs from his temples, he sat up and rubbed his eyes in an effort to push the pain of a whisky hangover back into his brain.

Swinging his legs around, he sat on the edge of the bed and tried to put his fragmented memories of yesterday back together again.

He remembered the whisky, the argument with the girl, the shotgun. He remembered the drugs and the van, and how angry she had been. But he had been right to bring them here, hadn't he? Science and knowledge were unquestionably more important than the individual. He was doing this for the good of the world. Pushing back the boundaries of human knowledge and bringing light into darkness.

He pressed his palms to his eyes and tried to ignore the voice that sounded like his mother, the voice telling him he was wrong and that he had done a bad thing.

Those poor children. You had no right, Jefferson. No right at all.

'You don't understand!' he shouted. 'You died! You went away and left me!'

He brushed the tears away with the back of his hand.

'What am I *supposed* to do?' he asked the empty room. 'I just want my dog back. Is that so much to ask? I just want to see Tansy one more time.'

Tansy. Of course.

How could he have forgotten?

That had been the whole point of it. And the children had agreed, hadn't they? Well maybe not the spoiled, nasty one. She had been too busy trying to make him angry, trying to ruin everything with her attitude. Her mind had been full of bad things, frightening things that he had transferred to the arrival cages for a closer look, although now he wished he hadn't. Same as he wished he'd left the thing from the boy's mind back where it was.

But the point was that the boy had understood the importance of what Jefferson was trying to do. He had helped him, attaching the electronic sensors to his head just the way Jefferson had shown him. And then Jefferson had gone to sleep and dreamed of . . . of what? Had he dreamed of Tansy? His head hurt and he couldn't be sure.

Jefferson put his head on one side and listened. The usual sounds from the forest. A jaybird calling to its mate. Bugs buzzing against the screen door. But nothing else. No sound of anyone moving around the kitchen, no kettle boiling, no one cutting bread or fixing a pot of coffee.

Jefferson felt the chill of anger in his blood. The boy had promised. Said he would help to bring Tansy back.

Sliding off the bed, Jefferson strode across the room and wrenched the door open. As he expected, the living room was empty. He remembered something else and checked all the rooms several times, not wanting to believe it, although he knew that it was true. He went to the kitchen table and shook his head, moving his papers, scanning the room, even dropping to his knees and peering with increasing desperation beneath the couch. But of course, it wasn't there. Not only had they left him, same as everyone did, but they had taken his shotgun too.

Jefferson swore, banging his fist on the table so that the papers jumped, some of them sliding off onto the floor. A thought occurred to him and he snatched his jacket from the back of the door and checked the pockets. When he found that the keys were gone, he knew that they had been to the out-house, to the place where yesterday's mistakes and secrets were kept, and he began to feel very afraid. But then a thought full of hope came shining through, because that was what all this had been about, hadn't it? Cal had promised he would find the dog and Jefferson was sure now that he wasn't a boy who would break his promises. He would have searched Jefferson's dreams and found Tansy, and brought her back to him. No doubt the girl in-terfered then, made him run away with her. But that was all right, wasn't it? Because Tansy was probably out there right now, waiting patiently for him, and they would be together again.

Everything would be all right.

In that moment of clarity, Jefferson's anger evap-orated like rain after a storm. He opened the back door and felt the sun warm on his face. As he walked along the path through the undergrowth, he listened for the tell-tale whines or barks that would let him know she was waiting for him.

But nothing yet.

Perhaps, he thought, they had tied her up or, more likely, left her in the arrival cage where she would be safe until he found her. He hoped that at least they had been thoughtful enough to leave her some food before they took off. The girl wouldn't have, of course; too busy thinking about herself. But he felt sure Cal would have done. He could tell just from the way he spoke about things that he knew what it was like to be alone in this world, understood the importance of reaching out to another soul when you had the chance.

Emerging from the clearing, Jefferson saw at once that the door had been left open and for a moment he felt his anger returning. Why were people never able to do things properly? If you unlocked a door and opened it, wasn't it obvious you needed to close it and lock it again when you left?

It was the girl again, he knew it. He could imagine Cal being careful, wanting to make sure that everything was just so, and her saying, *No, Cal, leave it, we have to get away from the crazy man.*

He wondered how she was liking it now.

Jefferson knew how confusing the forest could be if you didn't know your way around, every tree more or less the same, making you think you'd seen it a thousand times before. He imagined them stumbling through the night, becoming more and more lost, wondering if they would ever find their way out again.

Well, they wouldn't, Jefferson knew that much.

The forest was a hundred miles of wilderness that would swallow them without a trace. They would just be two more missing persons, two out of thousands in this sad, messed-up world, their pictures fading on posters and milk cartons before the world forgot about them altogether.

But then the thought came back to Jefferson that he had done a bad thing, that he should never have put them in his van.

'All right!' he said out loud, and then again, a little louder. 'All *right!*'

He had done it for the right reasons, he told himself. You couldn't make an omelette without breaking eggs, as his mother used to say.

It was a means to an end, and that end was bringing Tansy back.

And once she was back, then everything would be OK because she would come with him into the woods, just like she used to. They would find Cal and the girl and he would say to them, *Look at this, look at this good thing you have done*, and it would be like one of those fairy tales that his mother used to read to him on winter nights by the light of the fire, the ones where lots of terrible and frightening things happened but then good triumphed over evil and everything in the world was all right again.

Jefferson smiled.

He would be the author of a story with a happy ending.

'Tansy,' he called, stepping through the door into the cool shadows of the outhouse. 'Tansy, it's me. Where are you, girl? Hey, Tansy. Speak to me!'

Whether it was the heat, or the after-effects of the alcohol, Jefferson didn't know, but he began to feel distinctly queasy.

Why wasn't she answering?

The door of the arrival room had been left on the latch and he hurriedly walked in. The arrival cage was unlocked and the door was open.

The cage was empty.

'He didn't get her,' he whispered, hardly able to believe that the boy would let him down so badly. 'He didn't bring her back.' He walked across to the cage and slammed it angrily back on its hinges. But as he did so he noticed something caught on a piece of wire, poking out from the edge of the frame. Crouching down for a closer look, he saw that it was a tuft of fur, mottled with tiny patches of black.

'Oh, Tansy,' said Jefferson, pulling out the fur and holding it against his cheek. 'Tansy, you're here.'

He stood up and listened, full of anticipation. She had been here, in this cage, pulled from eternity through the gateway of his dreams. He was sure that, at any moment, he would hear the familiar barks and whines of the companion who had been away for so long.

'Tansy!' he called excitedly. 'Tansy, I'm coming!'

But as he walked out again, he glanced up the corridor and noticed that the other doors were open.

'No,' he muttered, suddenly anxious. 'No, no, no.'

He ran to the first room and saw that there was a trail of slime leading across the floor and, in the corner of the cage, a circular hole. He peered in and saw that the hole went straight down for about a metre before tunnelling off to the left.

'Oh no,' he said again. 'No, no.'

It occurred to him, as he checked the second cell and found the cage empty, that this was almost certainly the man's doing. When the man had first arrived from Cal's dream he had seemed temporarily stunned by the transition, and Jefferson had used the combination of his confusion and the shotgun to drag him out of the arrival cage and up the corridor, locking him in a cell until he could figure out what to do with him. But the man had come round fairly quickly after that, peering back at Jefferson through the spy hole until Jefferson wished he had never brought him here.

He had been too full of himself, hadn't he? Too caught up in the science of it, in the possibility of playing God and bringing a human back to life. But the moment the man smiled and said, 'I want the boy. Take me to the boy,' Jefferson knew he had made a mistake.

'Who are you?' he had asked.

The man had beckoned him nearer to the spy hole and in the gloom he was able to make out the neat, careful stitching along the seams of the man's jacket.

'I am the tailor,' the man whispered, 'and I have some cutting to do.'

Jefferson had walked away then, past the other rooms filled with things stolen from the girl's nightmares. But there was one important fact he had overlooked, of course; that although he could bring these creatures out of the darkness, he was unable to send them back again. He had given them life, and now he would have to live with the consequences.

But then Jefferson felt the softness of the dog's fur between his finger and thumb and remembered that, in the midst of all this mess, there was at least one good thing to come out of it.

Running back along the corridor, he stepped out into the sunshine.

'Tansy!' he called. 'Don't be frightened. It's me. You remember me, don't you, Tansy? Where are you?'

At first the sound didn't register, perhaps because the forest was always alive with the buzz and hum of insects. But then he noticed that the sound was unusually loud, and that it came from somewhere nearby.

Puzzled, Jefferson walked around the outside of the building, past the store that was half-stocked with logs for winter and beneath the branches of an apple tree that had sprung from the seeds of a discarded core.

As he turned the corner he gasped, his mouth wide open in horror.

Then, as his legs gave way, he leaned against the crumbling brickwork, sliding down until at last he was on his knees, turning his face to the wall so that he wouldn't have to see the cloud of green and gold flies, buzzing and settling upon the bloodied mass of fur that lay amongst the nettles and willow herb that grew along the edge of the forest.

TWENTY-FIVE

'I think it's our only option,' said Eden. 'If we follow the stream it should eventually take us down the mountain and back to the river. Which is where the campground is.'

'Yeah, but we don't know how far Jefferson took us, do we?' Cal waved his hand in an effort to disperse the midges that danced in front of his face. 'The campground could be a hundred miles from here.'

'Maybe. But at least if we get to the river we've got a chance of finding civilisation.'

She was right, of course. But the stream was where Cal had last seen the man, and he wasn't in too much of a hurry to run into him again. They had decided to walk back up the mountain at an angle, basing their plan on the fact that the man would have seen Cal running away from the stream and so

123

would probably expect him to carry on in that direction before attempting to head off down the mountain. So while the man set off on a false trail, they would be able to double back and make their way further east before heading down again once they had put some miles between them. But as they approached the stream Cal's fear returned, jangling his nerves as he remembered the look on the man's face and the water, dark with blood.

Eden saw him hesitate and put her hand on his arm.

'It's a big place, Cal. We've been walking for over an hour. If he was going to find us, he'd have found us by now.'

Cal clenched his fists as they walked by the edge of the stream, half expecting the man to appear at any moment. But as the trees thinned and the sun warmed his face, the feeling of danger lessened and Cal began to wonder if perhaps he had over-reacted.

This was America, he reminded himself. They played football in crash helmets. Their woods were full of poison ivy. They did things differently here. Sure, the guy had been dressed weirdly enough. But was it any weirder than some of the other people he'd seen through the window of the camper van, walking the backstreets or offering to wash the windscreen at junctions?

Like all the other strange stuff that had happened in the last twenty-four hours, he was beginning to think that maybe the trick was just to adapt to it and move on. But perhaps the strangest thing of all was that, for the first time in years, the unhappiness that had lain beneath the surface of everything he did was starting to dissolve. For a few brief moments, what had gone before and what lay ahead of him no longer seemed important; all that mattered was that he was here, now, walking in sunlight and listening to the water chatter across the stones.

'Hey, Cal.'

Eden's voice broke into his thoughts and he turned to see her standing with her hands on her hips, up to her ankles in the stream.

'Are you OK? You've gone pretty quiet.'

Cal nodded.

'Just thinking, that's all.'

'About what?'

Cal shrugged.

'I don't know. That I quite like it up here. You know. Away from everything.'

Eden looked at him, shielding her eyes from the sun.

'You *like* it?'

'Yeah. Kind of.'

'You realise we could be miles from the nearest

town? I mean, not just a few miles. Like fifty. A hundred, even.'

'Yeah, but you were in the Girl Scouts, weren't you? So maybe we can live off the land and hunt wild boar and stuff.'

Eden frowned.

'Are you kidding me?'

'I don't know. I just . . . I'm starting to feel like everything's going to work out OK.' He shrugged. 'Maybe it's just the after-effects of the stuff Jefferson put in our drinks.'

'Maybe,' said Eden. 'But whatever it is, hang on to it. Cos as my grandmother used to say, we ain't out of the woods yet.'

The stream meandered through the trees, at one point dropping through a narrow gully so that they were forced to clamber down its steep sides, stepping from stone to stone as they followed it between banks green with moss and ferns. Up ahead, Cal noticed several smaller streams cascading down and merging, increasing the volume of water so that the stream became broader and deeper, until at last it opened out into a clearing where a large woodland pool reflected the green pines surrounding it and the blue sky above.

They walked around the edge until they came to a place where the ground dropped away through the trees. A waterfall plunged hundreds of feet down the side of the mountain and far below Cal could see the silver glint of the river, winding its way through the valley. Beyond it, the forest covered the slopes of another mountain range, so that the landscape was clothed in a blanket of green.

'It's like something from a storybook,' said Cal.

'It's also a bit of a problem,' said Eden. 'There's no way we can climb down there.'

Cal looked at the sheer, dizzying drop and knew she was right. Trying to reach the river valley by that route was definitely not an option.

To the right of them, the mountain rose steeply again, making the descent even more dangerous. To their left it gradually curved towards the lower slopes, but that was far in the distance; in between were several miles of sheer rock face that would make it impossible to climb down with any degree of safety.

'We're going to have to go back, aren't we?' said Cal.

Eden nodded. 'It looks that way. Maybe we could cut through the woods a little earlier.'

'Maybe. But I think we should follow the river for some of the way. Help us keep our bearings.'

'Dammit.' Eden sat cross-legged beside the pool and rested her chin on her hands. 'I don't know about you, but I'm exhausted. What time do you think it is?'

Cal looked at the sun, high above the trees.

'One o'clock? Two, maybe?'

Eden rubbed sweat from her forehead and wiped it on her jeans.

'I don't suppose you have any food?'

'Let me check.'

Cal patted his pockets sarcastically.

'No, I don't think I have. But maybe that's because we left in a bit of a rush. What with you wanting to get away and everything.'

'Hey.' Eden looked at him sharply. 'You were the one who wanted to check on your friend's little doggy. You remember the guy I'm talking about. The one who drugged us, threw us in a van and stuck electrodes on our heads.'

Cal stared back at her, angry now.

'And whose idea was it to go into the woods? Not mine, that's for sure. I just went to do the washing-up. But you were all like, "Ooh, let's go and have an adventure. It'll be fun!"'

'Yeah, well, you didn't have to come, did you? But then, let me see, wait a minute, what was it you said? Oh yeah, that's right, people are always telling you, *Do this, Do that*. Well, no one's telling you what to do now, Cal. Least of all me.'

Eden stood up and threw a stone into the deepest part of the pool. 'From here on in, you can make you own decisions. And then maybe you'll start taking some responsibility for them. Because blaming other people, that's the coward's way out. I thought you were better than that. But obviously I was wrong.'

Eden turned and began walking back along the edge of the pool towards the forest. Cal felt bad then, not only because the things she said had hurt him, but because they were true.

'Where are you going?' he called, running to catch up with her.

Eden turned to him angrily.

'I don't know. But I was a Girl Scout, remember? I'm quite capable of doing this on my own.'

'I know you are,' said Cal, 'but I don't want you to. And I'm sorry.'

'For what?'

'For being all those things you said. And for being an idiot.'

Eden stopped walking then. She looked away from him, at the moss on the rocks and the reflections of the trees in the water. 'You're not an idiot, Cal,' she said quietly. 'And you don't need to be sorry. You just need to be . . . different.'

For a few moments, there was silence.

Then Cal untied his sweatshirt from around his waist and slipped his T-shirt over his head.

'OK,' he said. 'In that case, maybe I'll start by making a decision.'

Eden frowned.

'What kind of decision?'

'One based on the fact that I'm hot, I'm tired and my clothes are sticking to me.'

He took off his shoes, balanced them on a rock and began unbuttoning his jeans.

'Cal?' Eden stared at him uncertainly. 'What are you doing?'

'Like I said,' replied Cal, stepping out of his jeans to reveal a pair of blue boxer shorts, 'I've made a decision. And the decision is, I want to go swimming.'

As Eden put a hand up to her mouth to stifle a laugh, Cal stepped into the pool and waded in up to his knees. Then, before he could change his mind, he threw himself forward in a dive that took him down to the bottom of the pool, his fingers brushing the smooth stones before he splashed up to the surface again, the ice-cold water leaving him gasping for breath.

'You're crazy!' called Eden from the side of the pool. 'You know that, don't you?'

'Nah,' said Cal, dancing around in an effort to keep warm. 'It's called making a decision.'

He flipped over onto his back and kicked his legs so that spray skittered across the surface like diamonds.

'Come on,' he said. 'You know you want to.'

'Actually, I don't,' said Eden.

'Course you do,' said Cal. 'How often do you get to swim in a pool halfway up a mountain? Just think. Next time you're trailing around a dusty museum, do you really want to look back and think, I wish I'd done that?'

'All right, all right!' said Eden, kicking off her shoes and unbuttoning her jeans. 'But I'm telling you, if it's freezing, I'm going to come over there and stand on your head.'

Cal saw that she was laughing and it made him laugh too.

'You'll have to catch me first,' he said.

Eden was still smiling, right up until the moment the water reached her calves and her mouth formed a little O of shock. Then she recovered just enough to point a finger at him.

'OK, mister,' she said. 'Now you're gonna get what's coming to ya.'

And with that she threw herself forward and began swimming across the open water towards him.

Cal watched her long enough to realise what a

good swimmer she was – head down, breathing to the side – and then he was off, laughing and spluttering and kicking his legs in an effort to make it to the far side before she caught up with him. He almost made it, but with a couple of metres to go she grabbed his ankle, pulled him backwards and pushed him under the water. Cal opened his eyes and saw blurred stones and weeds waving in the current. Then her fingers dug into his sides and he burst through the surface, coughing and splashing his way to the shallows.

He sat on the stones for a while, catching his breath and watching her swim over.

'I warned you,' she said. 'You don't want to mess with me.'

Cal smiled.

'Yeah, you're a dangerous one. I'm just glad you ditched the shotgun.'

Eden sat next to him and waved her foot amongst the weeds.

'Cal?'

'Uh-huh?'

'Do you think we'll make it out of here?'

'Yeah. Don't you?'

'I'm worried about Jefferson. He ain't gonna be too happy when he wakes up and finds we've gone.'

Cal felt a pang of guilt then, and although he knew

it was crazy to feel sorry for a man who had got them into all this trouble, he couldn't help it.

'We got his dog back for him, didn't we? That was what he wanted.'

'Yeah but like you said, we got an angry version of it. I made Jefferson angry, he went to bed angry, and so he dreamed up an angry dog.'

'That might not be the reason.'

'It might not. But if the things that happen in the world can affect the way you feel inside, then the feelings you have inside can also affect what happens out in the world. I guess it's a two-way street.'

'How do you mean?' asked Cal.

'I mean, for instance, if something bad happens to you, it can make you feel horrible inside and that can affect the way you behave towards other people. And the way you behave towards other people can affect the way they behave towards you, which affects the way you are with them and so it goes, on and on. And then if you're not careful you can get stuck in one way of being for the rest of your life. That's probably why Jefferson's the way he is.'

'So we're stuck with what the world gives us, then,' said Cal. 'The world makes us who we are.'

'It can do,' said Eden, plucking a stone from the stream bed and throwing it into deeper water. 'But it doesn't have to.'

133

'Why not?'

'Because we can choose how we react to things. We can make our own decisions, remember?'

'OK,' said Cal. 'Then let's decide we're going to get out of here. Let's decide we're going to go home.'

Eden scooped up some water and cupped it in the palm of her hand.

'I'll drink to that,' she said.

TWENTY-SIX

It wasn't until the sun slipped behind the trees that Cal realised they were going to have to spend another night in the forest. His mood, which earlier on had been buoyant and hopeful, now faded with the dying sun. The insects quietened, the birds returned to their nests and the shadows lengthened beneath the pines.

'You know where we are, don't you?' asked Eden as the trees thickened around them.

'In a forest,' said Cal wearily. He was tired and hungry. They had shared a handful of red thimbleberries that Eden had found growing in a forest clearing, but that was all they had eaten since the previous day. They had been walking since first light and suddenly the effort of speaking seemed almost too much.

'Yeah, in a forest,' said Eden. 'In exactly the same place we started out.'

And as Cal followed her beneath a low branch he saw the shelter she had built the night before.

Eden picked up a stick and threw it as hard as she could through the trees. Cal listened to it clatter through the branches and heard the alarm call of a startled jay.

'I don't understand,' he said. 'How did we end up back here?'

'Let me give you a clue,' said Eden, smacking her hand against the trunk of a tree. 'They all. Look. The frickin'. Same.'

'Maybe we should just get some rest and wait until morning,' said Cal. Although he wasn't exactly keen on spending another night in the forest, his fear was tempered by exhaustion. The thought of lying down and sleeping for a few hours suddenly seemed very appealing.

'And then what, Cal? Do exactly the same thing to-morrow? Cos the way things are going, we're going to spend the rest of our lives running round in circles. That's if we don't get attacked by bears or something first.'

'Hey,' said Cal, putting a hand on her shoulder. 'I thought you were a Girl Scout.'

'Not any more.' Eden leaned back against a tree, folded her arms and slid down to the ground. 'I quit.'

'We'll be all right,' said Cal. 'Everything will be better tomorrow.'

Eden raised an eyebrow.

'You've changed your tune.'

Cal shrugged.

'It was just something someone said to me a couple of hours ago about choices and decisions. Can't remember who it was, though. Some girl or other.'

Eden managed a faint smile.

'She sounds like a right pain in the ass.'

'Totally.'

Cal stretched out a hand and helped her up.

'Promise me we'll get out of here tomorrow,' she said, resting her head on his shoulder.

'I promise,' said Cal.

For a moment, the world seemed to stand still.

And, just for a moment, Cal wished it would stay that way.

TWENTY-SEVEN

At first Cal thought it was Eden's breathing he could hear, the sound as faint as waves whispering to the shore. But when he opened his eyes and saw her sleeping silhouette he realised that the sound came from outside the shelter.

It was closer now, the soft, almost imperceptible sound of air flowing into lungs and out again.

'Eden,' he whispered. '*Eden*. Wake up.'

The sound stopped, to be replaced by a faint scratching, like a small creature searching for seeds amongst the branches.

Cal watched the pine needles tremble and he moved closer, hardly daring to breathe. A tiny grey speck appeared in the side of the shelter, a full stop in a jumble of green. Then the full stop grew, sliding towards him like a tiny mountain, and just as Cal realised that he was staring at the tip of a metal blade it twisted and retracted, leaving a small round hole. And as Cal watched, something moved in the centre of the hole and Cal saw that it was an eye, and it was staring directly into his own.

'Hello, Cal,' whispered a voice, thin as wood smoke. 'Shall we begin?'

Then the blades of the shears plunged through the weave of branches, their sharp edges ripping through Cal's sleeve and drawing a dark line of blood along his upper arm.

As Cal cried out and clamped his hand over the wound, Eden kicked at the other side of the shelter and pulled him through just as the blades thumped into the earth where he had been lying only seconds before.

Stars glittered overhead. Rolling onto his side, Cal saw the man standing beside the ruined shelter, opening and closing the shears as he stared at Cal through the gloom.

'Is that him?' whispered Eden.

'It's me he's come for,' said Cal as the man took a step towards them. 'Not you.'

Eden stared at him, not understanding. 'How do you know?'

Cal thought of the drawings and the nightmares that had haunted him for so long.

'I just do,' he said.

He looked at the man then, at the old-fashioned clothes, the top hat and the frock coat. And as the man smiled and took another step towards them, Cal did the bravest thing he had ever done in his life.

'Go,' he whispered, pushing Eden with the flat of his hand. '*Run.*'

If he was surprised at how fast she moved, how quickly she fled into the woods, then it was only momentary, soon to be replaced by the realisation that nothing now stood between him and the man who had pursued him through his nightmares.

'Please,' he said, clasping his hands together as if this might somehow make a difference. 'What do you want? What are you going to do to me?'

The man put his head on one side, like an adult addressing a small child.

'Oh dear,' he said. 'Are you afraid?' He opened the shears and closed them again, once, twice, as if to encourage an answer.

Cal felt the stars whirl above him; imagined he heard the whisper of dead things beneath his feet.

'Yes,' he said. 'Of course I'm afraid.'

The man smiled, as if this information pleased him.

'People who are afraid will often fight to stay alive,' he said, 'even if they know there is no chance of survival.'

He took the shears and rested the tips of the blades against his own chin, studying Cal with an amused expression.

'So tell me. Do you think you will fight?'

Cal shook his head, although not in answer to the question.

'You don't have to do this,' he said.

'Oh, but I do,' said the man. 'Answer the question.'

'Please,' said Cal.

'Answer the question,' repeated the man in a sing-song voice. 'Answer. The. Question.'

'I don't know,' said Cal.

'Well, then,' said the man, lowering the shears until they pointed straight at Cal's head. 'Let's find out, shall we?'

TWENTY-EIGHT

Cal felt his legs weaken and for a moment he was tempted to just give in, to fall to his knees, because the waiting was almost worse than what was coming.

'Why are you doing this?' he asked, his voice trembling.

'You know why,' said the man. 'I am doing it because you made me.'

'I *made* you?'

'That is correct. We all have a purpose, and yours was to give me life. You dreamed me into existence. Unfortunately for you, my purpose in life is to end yours. Don't you see, Cal? Such things cannot be resisted. They were written in the stars long before you or I ever came to be.'

'No,' said Cal, unable to tear his eyes from the

sharp blades as the man moved closer. 'That isn't true.'

'Oh but it is,' said the man, 'and you know it is. I'm part of you, Cal. I have been with you all along. I know all about your miserable existence, your feeling that the world never wanted you. And now you can see that it is true, Cal. An inescapable fact. The world wants you gone. And what the world wants, the world gets. You know I'm right, don't you, Cal? You *know* it.'

Cal remembered days spent watching other children from the corners of playgrounds, sitting in rooms with peeling wallpaper and staring at windows streaked with rain.

'Yes,' he said as the tears began to fall. 'It's true.'

'Then give me your hands,' said the man, nodding as if some kind of agreement had been made. He stepped forward, eyes gleaming, and opened the shears. 'Give me your hands, Cal. Let us put an end to this misery once and for all.'

Cal's lip trembled.

'Will it hurt very much?' he asked.

'Oh yes,' said the man. '*Very* much. But then it will be an end to the hurting for ever.'

Cal held out his hands and closed his eyes, because he didn't want to see how things would end.

It was written in the stars.

There was no way out.

But then, as the man took a deep, shuddering breath and the blades slid apart in a rasp of metal, Cal remembered the words Sarah had whispered in the dark of the camper van:

> Star light, star bright
> First star I see tonight
> I wish I may, I wish I might
> Have the wish I wish tonight

and suddenly he felt that the man was wrong, that there were things written in the stars better than he or the man could ever imagine. And the dark thoughts that whirled through his head were lit like a thundercloud which exploded into his fists and knocked the man sprawling to the floor. Then Cal was on top of him, punching him and crying out with fear and rage until at last he rolled off and the man lay on his back with blood on his lips, staring at the sky.

'Stay away from me,' said Cal, leaning against a tree. 'Just you stay away.'

Rubbing his bruised knuckles, he set off at a run through the trees, limping slightly but less afraid than he had been. He was shocked by his own violence and felt strangely detached from the world.

He wondered if the man was dead.

Were a few punches enough to kill someone?

Or had he struck his head on a rock when he fell?

Cal was still trying to remember if the man had been breathing, if there had been any obvious signs of life, when something hit him so hard in the back of the neck that his knees buckled and the ground hit him in the face like a slamming door.

TWENTY-NINE

The pain was excruciating, as if someone had tried to take his head off with an axe. Bright lights flashed behind his eyes and Cal groaned, breathing in the musty scent of damp earth. Then someone grabbed the back of his collar, pulled him to his knees and kicked him hard in the side.

'So you *do* like to fight,' said the man as a vicious punch sent Cal crashing into a tree. He tried to curl into a ball but the kicks came hard and fast, thudding into every part of his body. He could hear the man grunting with the effort and then his polished shoes smashed Cal's hands apart and when Cal opened his eyes the man was standing over him, shears dangling from his hand.

'This is fun,' he said. 'Do you want to play some more?'

Cal ran his tongue over swollen lips and tasted the

blood in his mouth. His left eye was already closing and his body ached all over.

'No,' he said. 'I don't want to play any more.'

'Then give me your hands,' said the man. 'Give me your hands like I told you in the first place.'

'Why are you doing this?' whispered Cal.

The man crouched beside him, made a show of turning his head and cupping his ear.

'Hmm? What's that you say?'

Cal coughed, his spit strawberry red.

'I said, why are you doing this?'

The man tutted and shook his head.

'Don't tell me you've forgotten.'

'Forgotten what?'

'The nursery rhyme. You know the one.'

And in that moment, it all came back.

He was four years old. He had been awake for hours, crying softly and sucking his thumb because the house mother had read them a story about a boy who was lost and had found his way home again. And for the first time Cal had realised that he was alone in the world, that no one would ever come looking for him and that he would never find his way home again because home did not exist. And while he was snuffling and sucking his thumb, one of the older boys had thrown a shoe at him to shut him up, but this had only made things worse.

'If we read you a story, Cal, will you go to sleep?'

Cal had looked up to see two of the older boys crouching next to his bed. One of them held a book and the other was shining a torch on it. He turned the torch on Cal and asked, 'Well? Are you going to answer the question?'

Cal took his thumb out of his mouth, nodded and put it back again. People were being kind to him and it was a new sensation.

'This is the story about what happens to little boys who suck their thumbs.'

The boys were grinning now, trying not to laugh.

'Do you want to hear it?'

Cal wasn't sure that he did, but he nodded because the boys were older and he wanted to please them.

'The Story of Little Suck-a-Thumb,' read the first boy.

> One day Mamma said, 'Conrad dear,
> I must go out and leave you here.
> But mind now, Conrad, what I say,
> Don't suck your thumb while I'm away.'

'Are you listening, Cal?' asked the other boy. 'Are you listening to this?'

And Cal had nodded, jamming his thumb further into his mouth and curling his index finger around his nose for comfort.

'The great tall tailor always comes
To little boys who suck their thumbs;
And ere they dream what he's about,
He takes his great sharp scissors out,
And cuts their thumbs clean off – and then,
You know, they never grow again.'

The boy stopped and stared at Cal by the light from the torch. 'This is a true story, Cal. You know that, don't you?'

Cal nodded again, shrinking further beneath the grey blanket.

Mamma had scarcely turned her back,
The thumb was in, Alack! Alack!
The door flew open, in he ran,
The great, long-legged scissor-man.
Oh! children, see! the tailor's come
And caught out little Suck-a-Thumb.
Snip! Snap! Snip! the scissors go;
And Conrad cries out 'Oh! Oh! Oh!'
Snip! Snap! Snip! They go so fast,
That both his thumbs are off at last.

'Do you think he'll die, Cal?' whispered the boy as he looked up from the book. 'Do you think he'll bleed to death?'

But Cal was too frightened to say anything.

Mamma comes home: there Conrad stands,
And looks quite sad, and shows his hands;
'Ah!' said Mamma, 'I knew he'd come
To naughty little Suck-a-Thumb.'

'Look, Cal,' said the other boy, forcing Cal to sit up.
'Look at the picture.'

He shone his light onto the book and Cal saw the man
flying through the doorway dressed in a dark green jacket
and shiny black shoes. His reddish-brown hair streamed
behind him and his top hat tumbled from his head as he
snipped at the boy's outstretched thumbs with a pair of
giant shears and the boy's blood splashed down upon the
carpet.

As Cal trembled beneath the sheets he heard the click
of the torch being turned off and then the low, threatening
whispers.

'He's waiting for you, Cal. Did you know that? He's
waiting outside the window, listening to see if anyone is
crying. So I should be very quiet from now on, Cal. Be
very quiet and take your thumb out of your mouth. Or you
know what will happen. You know what will happen . . .'

THIRTY

The creak of the shears opening and closing brought Cal back to the present. And as he stared at the man who had stalked him through his nightmares, he was almost glad that the waiting would soon be over. At last he would be able to sleep for ever, sleep without waking and calling for someone who would never come.

'You see, Cal?' the man whispered. 'You've always known I would come for you in the end.'

The man rested the tips of the shears on Cal's head and narrowed his eyes.

'Now get on your knees.'

Cal knelt on the carpet of pine needles, pressing his hands together like a holy man at prayer.

'No one ever loved you, Cal. Even your little friend ran off and left you, didn't she? But not me, Cal. Because you made me, didn't you? You created me so that I could bring all this sadness to an end. Sharp, quick and easy, that's how I work. Then no more pain, Cal. Do you understand me? No more pain and no more hurt.'

Cal's vision was blurred, partly because of the tears and partly because the world was unreal to him now, a trick that had been played upon his senses to make him believe he might one day find a place in it.

'Thumbs are for nursery rhymes. Give me your hands, Cal. Now that I'm here, we're going to do things properly.'

As Cal held out his hands the man's voice became softer, almost paternal.

'That's a good boy, Cal.'

The creak of the shears opening.

'Shhh, don't cry now.'

The edges of the blades, pressing against his skin.

'You're a good boy, Cal. Such a good boy . . .'

A loud crack echoed through the forest and suddenly the pressure on Cal's wrists disappeared.

Cal opened his eyes to see the man sink to his knees with a look of utter bewilderment on his face. The shears were on the ground in front of him and as he raised a hand to the side of his face there was another loud crack and he fell sideways into a tree.

'Take *that*, you scary-ass lunatic.'

Stepping out of the shadows, Eden stood behind him with a thick branch held tightly in both fists.

'Get up, Cal,' she said. 'Get up and let's get the hell out of here.'

Cal stared open-mouthed, first at Eden and then at the man crumpled against the tree like a pile of dirty washing.

'You came back,' he said.

'Well, of course I came back,' said Eden. 'Did you really think I'd leave you alone with this nut-job?'

At the sound of Eden's voice, the man raised his head and took a deep, shuddering breath. He pressed the flats of his hands against his head and gave it a little twist, as if fixing it back in place. Eden raised her stick, gripping it so hard that her knuckles stood out like pebbles beneath the skin.

'Don't try anything,' she said, 'or I'll give you another.'

The man stared at her for a few moments and then started to chuckle, quietly at first, then louder and louder as if in response to a joke that only he could hear.

'You'll give me another,' he repeated. 'Oh, that's very good, that is. Very good indeed.'

He clasped his knees and began to rock back and forth, shaking his head from side to side. 'She'll give me another,' he chuckled. 'She'll give me another.'

He threw back his head and cackled, pausing only to catch his breath before blowing fresh gales of laughter up into the treetops.

'Come on,' said Eden, looking at the man in disgust. 'Let's go.'

Immediately, the man was on his feet again.

'What's the matter?' he asked, pressing a finger to his chin. 'Don't you get it?'

His smile grew wider as he held out his finger and danced it back and forth in front of his face.

'Don't – You – Get – It?'

'Get what?' said Eden, curling her lip. 'There's nothing to get, y'smiley-faced freak.'

'Smile and the world smiles with you,' said the man, stepping closer. 'Weep and you weep alone. So what's it to be? Hmm?'

His finger continued to dance between them.

'Laugh or cry? Live or die?'

Too late, Cal saw his eyes dart towards the shears and Eden must have seen it too because she moved forward and swung her stick at the man's head.

But this time the man was too quick for her.

With astonishing speed he ducked low to the ground and as the stick swished harmlessly through the air he made a grab for the shears.

Eden was momentarily caught off balance and as she stumbled backwards he wrenched the stick from her grasp and flung it to the ground, striking her hard across the face with the back of his hand.

The force of the blow knocked her backwards and she cried out in pain as her head hit the ground.

'Oh yes, yes, yes!' cried the man, twirling the shears triumphantly above his head. 'Down they tumble, daughters, sons, down they tumble, every one.' He moved forward until he was standing above Eden, holding the shears by the tips of his fingers and dangling the blades above her face.

'Awww, she's not laughing,' he said in mock concern as Eden stared up at the shears. 'Perhaps I should explain the joke?'

He glanced at Cal with a look of amusement and then turned his attention back to Eden.

'You could have lived, you see. All you had to do was run away and save yourself. But oh no. You came back because you believed the old lie. The one that says goodness and love will always triumph in the end.'

The man looked at Cal, and at the trees, and at the blackness of the sky.

'The bindweed chokes the rose, the flies infect the wound, the lion devours the foal. Look around and you will see that there is no such thing as goodness; there is no such thing as love.'

The man waved the shears in an arc above his head, signifying the world and everything in it.

'That's the joke, you see? Strength is all that matters. Strength, and the knowledge that all things must come to an end. As you are about to discover.'

The man drew himself up to his full height, a terrible smile on his face as he lifted the shears ready to plunge them into Eden's heart. But Cal was filled with rage for all that would be lost and when Eden screamed he threw himself into the flash of shears, and then fear blurred into a confusion of darkness and blood.

Then they were running away through the forest and all they could hear was a screaming in the trees, and neither could be sure if the sound was human or animal, or if there was any difference.

THIRTY-ONE

They were still running when the first forks of light-ning crackled across the sky, thunder rumbling around the mountains like artillery fire. Seconds later the rain began, a soft pattering at first, then quickly turning to fat droplets that splashed through the trees and soaked the dry ground beneath. As dark thunderheads filled the sky Cal realised that, for the first time since arriving in Montana, he was actually shivering. Eden caught hold of his shirt and pulled him back, leaning against a tree to catch her breath.

'We can't just keep running,' she said. 'We need to stop and think.'

Cal was so fired up that he could have kept run-ning all night. But he saw that Eden was exhausted, resting her forehead against the tree as the rain ran down her face.

'I'm frightened,' she said. 'I don't think I can do this any more.'

'We have to,' said Cal. 'If we don't, we're dead.'

A succession of flashes lit up the sky and he saw the silhouettes of trees and the mountains beyond.

'We're going to get out of here, and we're going to do it tonight.'

Eden nodded, wanting to believe it as much as he did.

'Do you think you killed him?' she asked.

'I doubt it,' said Cal. 'He seems to be indestructible.'

He saw the blood on his hands and bent down and wiped them in the dirt. Rain rattled through the branches, stinging his face. He had been surprised at the way the man had fallen so easily. He remembered pulling the shears from the man's grasp and throwing them into the trees before punching him to the ground. Then the blood was warm on his hands, and the man lay awkwardly beneath the trees, staring up at the sky.

'Do you think he was right?' Cal asked.

'About what?'

'About strength being all that matters.'

Eden shook her head.

'Don't feel bad,' she said. 'If you hadn't stopped him, we'd both be dead.'

'But that means he *was* right,' said Cal. 'It means we're no different from plants or insects or anything else. Survival of the fittest. All we care about is staying alive.'

'That's not true,' said Eden. 'You could have run away and saved yourself. But you didn't, did you? You stayed, Cal. You stayed and you saved me.'

Cal shrugged.

'No more than you did for me.'

'That's what I'm saying, Cal. Look, maybe the world doesn't give a damn about any of us. But that doesn't stop us looking out for each other, does it? It doesn't stop us doing what we think is right.'

Cal watched jagged forks of lightning flicker across the sky.

'I don't know what to believe,' he said. He bunched his fists, pressing them to his eyes as the thunder echoed around the valley below. 'I don't know anything, Eden. I don't know what's real any more.'

'Yes you do,' said Eden, pulling his hands down and taking them in her own. 'Look at me, Cal. I'm real, aren't I?'

She led him across to a tree and pressed his hands against the bark.

'This tree is real. So is the rain, and the lightning, and the forest, and the whole of this crazy world that we're in. That man back there might have stepped out of your dreams, but he was real enough to hurt us, that's for sure. And like you said, Cal, we're going to get out of here. We're going back to a place where no one tries to hurt us any more. OK?'

Cal rested his head against the tree because he wanted to know that it was still solid, that the world had not dissolved.

'We'll never make it down to the valley in this weather,' he said. 'Maybe we should try and find our way back to the house.'

'Cal, we've just escaped from one psychopath. Let's not go looking for another one.'

'Jefferson's not a psychopath.'

'Don't even start,' said Eden, running a hand through her wet hair.

'I'm just saying we should go back and get our bearings. See if we can find out where we are.'

'Oh, like he's going to let us do that. Just walk right in there and help ourselves to his map collection.'

'Maybe not. But you've seen his place. The binoculars, guns and all the rest of it. He goes out, Eden. And when he does, that's when we go in.'

'And do what, exactly?'

'And find out where we are. You said you could drive, didn't you?'

'Yeah, but we tried that, remember? I couldn't find the keys.'

'But maybe that's because they were still in his pocket. Maybe now we've gone he'll have put them back in a drawer or wherever it is he keeps them.'

'That's a lot of maybes, Cal.'

'No, it stands to reason. He's not going to take his keys out hunting with him, is he? He's not going to risk dropping them somewhere in the middle of the wood.'

'But who says he's going out hunting?'

'He has to eat. Look, I know there are no guarantees, Eden. But at some point he's got to go out. And I seriously think it's our best chance of getting out of here.'

Eden chewed her lip and shivered.

'Yeah, well, maybe. But I don't like the sound of the hunting part. I mean, you know who he could be hunting for, right?'

'All the more reason for us to be out of these woods. The stream was on our right when came down the mountain, so as long as we keep it on our left, we should be heading in the right direction.'

In spite of the rain, Eden smiled.

'Are you sure *you* weren't in the Girl Scouts?'

'Dyb, dyb, dyb,' said Cal, grinning and making a three-fingered salute.

'OK, now you're just being weird. Sometimes I think you're completely—'

But Eden stopped mid-insult as a look of pure terror crossed her face. Beneath his feet, Cal felt a strange vibration in the earth.

'What is it?' he asked. 'What's the matter?'

But Eden just shook her head and clutched at his arm.

'It's coming,' she said. 'It's coming for me.'

THIRTY-TWO

'What?' asked Cal. 'What's coming?'

'*Shhh!*' hissed Eden, staring around like a frightened animal. 'We have to be quiet or it'll find us.'

Cal wanted to ask again *what* would find them, but he could see she was almost out of her mind with terror so he followed her gaze to the source of the tremor, which appeared to have moved a few metres in front of them. The earth trembled like a railway platform before the train arrives.

'What is it?' he whispered. 'What's going on?'

'You've had your nightmare,' said Eden. 'This one's mine.'

Cal saw something move in the trees and then a young mule deer emerged from the shadows with its nose twitching. As the earth shuddered again the deer pricked up its ears and stamped nervously, breath steaming in the damp night air.

'Whatever you do, don't move,' whispered Eden. 'That's what it's come for. It can sense the vibrations through the earth.'

Cal was still trying to figure out what she meant when the ground behind the deer suddenly cracked in two and a line of earth streaked across the forest towards it, like an invisible plough carving its way through the soil. As the frightened animal turned to run, the ground beneath it erupted and a long, worm-like creature with white, sightless eyes came squirming out of its newly formed burrow, testing the air with its head until it brushed against the deer's leg. Immediately, the creature's face split open to reveal slime-covered jaws that snapped shut on the animal's hind leg and dragged it struggling down into the earth.

It was over in seconds.

One moment the deer was there; the next it was gone, leaving only a dark hole and the sound of rain, dripping from the trees.

Cal stared at the line of earth and turned to Eden in disbelief.

'What the *hell* was that?'

'I've been having nightmares about it ever since I was a kid,' whispered Eden, unable to tear her gaze from the dark hole beneath the pines. 'But it can't be real, can it? I mean, it was just a dream.'

'I think we know the answer to that,' said Cal. 'But what *was* it?'

Eden put her hands over her eyes.

'I don't even want to think about it.'

'You have to,' said Cal, 'and then you have to tell me. Because if we're going to get out of here, we have to figure out a way of dealing with it.'

'But you saw what it did,' said Eden, close to tears. 'How the hell do we deal with something like that?'

'All right,' said Cal, 'just calm down and breathe.' He placed a hand on her shoulder and took a deep breath, encouraging her to do the same.

Eden leaned against the tree and looked over her shoulder, as if half expecting the creature to resurface.

'It's all right, it's gone,' Cal said. 'The deer will keep it busy for a while.'

He was aware that he sounded braver than he felt. But he knew that he had to try to control his fears for both their sakes.

'So, come on. Tell me about this dream.'

Eden wiped her eyes and Cal couldn't tell whether it was because of the rain or because she had been crying.

'It started when I was about six years old. I'd been

watching this cartoon on TV, something about some kids who were exploring a jungle where no one had ever been before. And I remember thinking it was kind of cool, because there were all these colourful plants and it seemed like such a beautiful place.'

'Sounds OK so far,' said Cal.

'That part was fine,' said Eden. 'But then the music changed, you know, to those creaky violins, and I could tell right away something bad was going to happen. And I wanted to go and find my mom, but I couldn't tear myself away from the TV. So I just kept right on watching.'

She stared into the distance as if she was watching a movie, replaying the whole thing in her mind.

'Then they came to a garden with a goat tethered to a tree in the middle, and it was surrounded by high stone walls. And the oldest kid pointed to a little pile of earth next to the wall, like a mole had been there or something. But then the camera zoomed in close and it started to grow real fast, and there was this rumbling sound . . .'

'Like just now,' said Cal.

'Yeah, just like that,' said Eden. 'And then it suddenly drilled its way across the yard and pulled the goat down into its burrow. It was the scariest thing I'd ever seen and I've had nightmares about it ever since. I must have had one at Jefferson's place, what with the drugs and all. That's when Jefferson must have lifted it from my mind.'

'But what happened in the end?' asked Cal. 'How did they deal with it?'

'I don't remember,' said Eden. 'I just remember it was able to track them down by sensing the vibrations when they walked. Which is what scared me more than anything. Because there was nowhere to hide.'

They listened in silence for a while, but all they could hear was the rain and the distant rumble of thunder.

'The storm's moving away,' said Cal, looking up at the sky. 'If we're going to make it to the house, then maybe we should get going.'

'Cal!' hissed Eden as he started to walk away. 'What are you doing?'

'I'm going to the house,' replied Cal. 'Like we agreed, remember?'

'But didn't you hear what I said? That thing can *sense* us. You saw what it did to the deer. If we start walking it's going to hear us and hunt us down. Do you want to be torn apart?'

'No I don't,' said Cal. 'But neither do I want to stay here for the rest of my life.'

'So you're just going to walk out there and let it kill us?'

Cal looked at her.

'Honestly?' he said. 'I don't know what I want to do. But I do know that we're going to die if we stay here with no shelter and nothing to eat or drink. So I say we have to take our chances and go for it.'

'But I'm scared,' said Eden quietly. 'I'm really, really scared.'

'I know,' said Cal, walking back to her. Then, as she began to cry for the first time since he had met her, Cal put his arms around her and rested his chin on the top of her head. 'Hey, come on,' he said. 'That thing just ate, remember? By the time it's ready for dessert, we'll be long gone.'

Eden pressed against him for a while longer until he added, 'Am I right?' and then she nodded and pulled away.

'I guess so,' she said, and Cal could see that she was still afraid but trying to be brave. 'Thank you, Cal.'

And although Cal was afraid too, he felt stronger than before.

'Just take it slow and quiet,' he said. 'We'll be out of here before you know it.'

Thirty-Three

As the storm raged outside, Jefferson placed the oil lamp in the middle of the table before pulling the faded brown photo album out of the bookcase. He sat down and tried to remember a time in his life when he had been happy.

Starting at the back, he looked at the pictures of him and Tansy, the last episodes of his life ever to be captured on camera. He was smiling then, but his happiness had been merely a rainbow of oil on the surface of dark waters. It was tempered by the knowledge that, in all probability, Tansy would die before him and he would be left alone in the world once more.

Turning to the front of the album, he saw the photograph of himself with his mother, the one he knew so well. The pair of them were standing together in the garden with a backdrop of roses and apple blossom, her wearing a straw hat and carrying a basket of flowers, him clutching a crumpled copy of *New Scientist*.

He knew, looking at the photograph, that just two days later he would be the happiest he had ever been in his life and that, like everything else in this world, his happiness would turn to dust.

He was seventeen years old. He had always been a loner, always the last one to leave the library at the end of the day.

'Time to go home now, Jefferson,' the librarian would say as the caretaker put the chairs on the tables and swept the floor around him. 'The books will still be here tomorrow.'

She was right, of course. Which was probably why Jefferson liked books more than people. Books were dependable things, full of facts that said this is how the world is. They never tried to confuse you by hiding what was inside. Books had no secrets. You could just open them up and look right in. And when you went back to them again they were always there, exactly where you left them.

Besides, Jefferson didn't need friends because his mother had told him that they would only distract him from his studies.

'Hard work and dedication. Those are the only things that will get you anywhere in this world,' she told him.

'Make me proud of you, Jefferson. Make me proud of who you are.'

And on that day, that summer day when the sky was bluer than the ocean and the handrails in the school yard were too hot to touch, he had walked out of the Principal's office with a smile on his face and a letter in his hand that told him the future was his for the taking.

He had run down the drive then, past the library where the librarian had adjusted her bifocals and tried to discern why he had not taken his usual path past the carefully planted shrub beds to the library entrance. She had half wondered to herself whether he might be sick, but the uncharacteristic smile on his face suggested otherwise, so she contented herself with the task of cataloguing the non-fiction section, reassuring herself that tomorrow everything would be back to normal. She would speak to Jefferson as he painstakingly scribbled his notes in a cheap, dime-store notebook and no doubt discover some ordinary, mundane reason for his unexplained absence.

But the reason was neither ordinary nor mundane, and as Jefferson walked out of the school gates and through the suburban streets with their carefully tended lawns, their white picket fences and their back-yard basketball hoops, he had a sense of a world rearranging itself around him, all the pieces clicking neatly into place.

Looking back on it now, Jefferson saw with sudden

clarity that this was the one moment in his life when he had been truly happy. The moment when all the setbacks and difficulties in the years leading up to it had suddenly seemed no more than tests; obstacles along a winding path that had led at last to a straight road, stretching far ahead of him. A road that would lead to a place where no one would ever laugh at him again, where people would marvel at his achievements and everyone would agree that Jefferson Boyd was a person who was going places.

And his mother.

His mother would be so proud.

Clutching the letter to his chest, Jefferson had stopped at the store to buy his mother some flowers. It was, after all, a celebration, and as he paid for them he imagined her fussing over their arrangement, picking out her favourite vase before placing it on the dresser by the window.

Taking the short-cut through the park, past the women who watched the swings tick the days of motherhood away, Jefferson hurried down the street and saw that the screen door was open and the front porch was empty. He thought this unusual because his mother was always there looking out for him, waiting on the porch swing for the moment when he would turn the corner and come back into her world again. But then he remembered, of course, that she wouldn't be expecting him yet because he always stayed at the library until late. It was unseasonably hot, even for July, and she had probably gone inside to prepare a jug of iced lemonade.

The door creaked on its hinges as Jefferson pushed it open, bluebottles buzzing around the screens. He heard the swish of the ceiling fan and the hum of the refrigerator.

'Mom?' he called, placing the flowers on the drainer and reaching for her favourite vase. 'It's me, Jefferson. I came home early.' He wandered into the living room and saw that the cushions were all straightened up, same as they had been when he left that morning. Figuring she must be in the bedroom, he went into the hallway and called up the stairs.

'Mom, come on down, will ya? I got something to show you.'

Still no answer.

He smiled to himself, guessing she'd gone upstairs for a nap and fallen asleep in the heat.

Even now, more than thirty years later, Jefferson could recall every detail: the worn carpet, the smell of her perfume, the ticking of the clock in the hall.

He found her lying by the bed. She looked as though she was fast asleep, although according to the paramedics who had arrived within minutes of his frantic phone call, she had been dead for several hours. It was a heart attack, they explained, apparently brought on by a combination of the heat and the effort of climbing the stairs. 'I'm sorry,' said the older paramedic as they carried her out of the house for the last time. 'It must be a terrible shock.'

After he had watched the ambulance drive away, Jefferson had walked back into the house that suddenly seemed so empty and sat down at the kitchen table.

He had stared at the letter for a long time, the letter offering him a scholarship to Harvard, the letter that she would never see. And it was as if at that moment his heart, like hers, became something solid and unmoving; calcified in an instant by the realisation that he had been cast adrift on an endless sea, and there was no one left to save him.

Jefferson closed the photograph album, opened the door and walked out into the storm. He didn't mind that it was raining, or that he was cold, or that his clothes were soaked through. As lightning crackled and thunder rumbled around the mountains, he walked across to where Tansy was buried and fell to his knees beside the fresh mound of earth. He thought of all the years he had spent, working alone in the early hours, trying to bring back what was lost. But the only thing his efforts had brought him was isolation and ridicule. And now, now that he had actually found a way of doing what everyone had told him was impossible, his chance of happiness had been snatched away. And not only that, but in his excitement he had opened a dangerous gateway and filled the world with things that did not belong.

Suddenly the years of frustration and sadness rose up inside him and he cried out to the sky in anger and in sorrow.

'It's not my fault!' he shouted. 'I only wanted to make things better!'

But he knew in his heart that he had only succeeded in making them worse.

'It's not my fault!' he shouted again. 'It's not – my – fault!'

He stared at the soil that was already turning to mud and, as the rain ran down his face, his sorrow became anger instead.

'All right,' he said. 'We'll see about this. We'll just see.'

Then he went back inside the house and opened the shoebox where he hid his .38 revolver. He took out six bullets, loaded them into the chamber and snapped it shut.

Then he opened the door and walked outside, only this time he didn't stop.

He just kept on walking, through the rain and into the shadows of the forest.

Thirty-Four

As suddenly as it had started, the rain stopped and the skies cleared to reveal a bright crescent moon above the trees.

Cal shivered and tried to concentrate on walking as softly as he could. It reminded him of a game the other children played at school once in a while – Grandmother's Footsteps or something like that. One person was chosen to stand at the front with their eyes closed and the others had to creep up on them without being heard. The only difference was, if you got caught, you had to go and sit on the side until the game was over and then you got another go.

Here, there would be no second chances.

So although Cal was exhausted, fear kept him alert. His hearing became sensitive to the smallest of sounds until every breath, every falling raindrop, became a piece of information that could save his life.

But it was Eden who heard it first.

'Cal!' she hissed, grabbing his arm. Cal heard the faint rustle of branches from somewhere behind him but as he turned, the sound stopped.

'Did you hear it?'

Cal nodded. He felt as if they were taking part in some kind of cruel game which occasionally allowed them to believe there was hope of survival, when in fact there was none.

They listened for a time without moving, trying to locate the source of the sound.

'Can you hear it now?' Cal whispered.

Eden shook her head.

'But there was definitely something there.'

'I know. I heard it too.'

Another sound, like a foot scraping the earth. A slight tremor of the branches, less than five metres in front of them.

'OK,' said Cal quietly, keeping his eyes on the shadows beneath the trees. 'No sudden movements.' He touched Eden's arm and realised that she was trembling. 'We'll just move back and go a different way.'

He stepped back and Eden followed, matching his footsteps as they slowly moved away. Unable to shake the feeling that something was watching them, Cal concentrated on staying silent and gradually increasing their distance from whatever was lurking in the shadows. He felt the branches brush against his head and knew that if they could just get a little further into cover they might have a chance.

But then he heard Eden whimper and turned to see her standing with her hand over her mouth and her eyes wide open, staring straight ahead. As he followed her gaze there was a squelching sound and the ground broke open to reveal what appeared to be a dark hood emerging from a layer of soft mud.

'What is it?' Cal whispered as two deathly-white hands reached out of the hole, their fingers feeling around the edges for firmer ground.

'They come for me at night,' said Eden, her voice shaking as the figure pulled itself from the thick mud which oozed out onto the dry ground around it. 'They're the dark men.'

Cal watched the figure claw its way out of the mud and saw how the mud seemed to slide off it to reveal a figure dressed in a hooded cloak, its face almost completely hidden except for the dull red glow of its eyes.

'Dark *men*?' asked Cal, but as Eden nodded he saw that all around them the earth was rising, forming circular crusts which burst open to reveal more ghostly figures clawing their way out into the night.

Cal swore as the first one began running towards them through the trees. But before it could reach them the ground shook and a furrow of earth appeared on the surface, lengthening and speeding towards it. Then the ground erupted and Cal saw the huge worm coiling around the man's legs, dragging him down to the accompaniment of grunts and screams.

As the other figures fell back, Cal pushed Eden through the trees and together they ran blindly beneath thickening branches towards the place in the woods where their nightmares had first become real.

Thirty-Five

'There it is,' said Eden as they stumbled through a gap in the trees. 'I can see a light.'

Cal looked behind him and imagined he could hear the sound of breathing, of things moving steadily through the trees towards them.

'We need to get inside,' he said, 'and we need to do it now.'

'What about Jefferson?'

Cal looked at the house and saw that the only light was the one above the door.

'Probably asleep. And he told me he never locks the doors. No need.' Cal looked over his shoulder. 'Until now, anyway.'

'What if he hears us?'

'Then maybe he'll help us.'

Cal saw that Eden was still undecided.

'Look, if he wakes up, we'll deal with it. Otherwise

we find the keys, you drive the van and we get the hell out. OK?'

'OK.'

They ran across the clearing to the back of the house and opened the door. The house was in darkness but as Cal fumbled for the light switch Eden pulled his hand away.

'There's a flashlight in the kitchen drawer,' she said. 'I saw it when I was looking for the keys.'

Cal retrieved it and shone it at Jefferson's door to check that it was closed. He made a quick sweep of the kitchen table, but the keys were nowhere in sight.

He nodded towards Jefferson's denim jacket hanging on the back of the door and held the light steady while Eden checked the pockets, but they were empty. With increasing desperation they checked all the cupboards and drawers, Cal half-expecting the rattle of cutlery to wake Jefferson, but the door to his room remained firmly closed.

'They're not here,' said Eden at last. 'They must be in his room.'

Cal shone the torch at her.

'You want to go and check?'

'Not without some help.'

Cal swept the torch beam around the room one more time.

'OK,' he said. 'Let's do it.'

He walked towards Jefferson's bedroom door, picking out the handle in a circle of light. Then he switched off the torch and slowly turned the handle, wincing as the mechanism creaked. When the door was open a crack he listened for the sound of breathing, but there was none.

'Get ready,' he whispered.

Then he pushed the door open and turned on the torch.

The first thing he noticed was the picture of Jefferson's dog on his nightstand. The second was the skein of wires which ran across the surface of the walls before disappearing into the roof and beneath the floorboards. And the third was that Jefferson's bed was empty.

There was an old dresser in the corner and Eden pulled open the drawers, but all she found was a threadbare sweater and a few crumpled T-shirts.

'Do you think he's still here?' she asked.

'Doesn't look like it,' said Cal, tossing her the torch before walking to the window and peering through the blinds. 'And neither should we be.'

'But what if he's taken the van?'

They stared at each other for a moment and then ran back through the living room and out of the door.

'I see it,' breathed Cal with relief as they clattered

around the side of the outbuildings to find the van half hidden behind some bushes. As they got closer Cal saw that beyond the bushes was a narrow dirt track, leading away through the trees.

'That's it,' said Eden. 'That's our way out of here.'

'But it could be miles,' said Cal. 'I don't suppose they taught you how to hot-wire a car in the Girl Scouts?'

Eden stood on tiptoes and peered through the driver's window.

Then she gasped.

'Cal! Look!'

She pulled open the door, gave a little whoop of triumph and held up the keys.

'They were in the ignition.'

She leaned over the seats and opened the passenger door.

'I don't believe it,' said Cal, shaking his head as he climbed in beside her. 'He must leave them there the whole time. I mean, who's going to come all the way out here to nick a van?'

Eden smiled and started the engine.

'We are,' she said.

*

For the first few minutes, Eden's driving made Cal

wonder whether she had ever been behind the wheel of a car in her life. The van juddered, the gears grated and whenever they got up speed she steered so close to the trees that Cal found himself pulling his elbows away from the window in case they were taken off along with the door.

'Takes a bit of getting used to,' said Eden, leaning forward and peering at the road ahead. 'But I think I've got the hang of it now.'

The headlights picked out a fallen branch in the road and Eden swerved so violently that Cal banged his head against the side window.

'I'm glad to hear it,' he said, pulling his seat belt tighter.

He checked the mirror to see if anything was following them but the road was hidden by the dark and the dust from the wheels.

'We're doing it, Cal,' said Eden, changing up a gear. 'We're actually doing it. We're going home.'

Cal could hear the relief in her voice, but as he looked at the glare of the headlights, he couldn't help wondering if that was all this was – a small patch of brightness on a long dark road. He knew in his heart that the man with the shears was part of him, just as the dark figures that pursued them were a part of Eden. That although they had run away this time, there was a chance that those things would be waiting for them, somewhere down the road.

'Are you OK?' asked Eden. 'You've gone very quiet.'

'Just tired, I guess. It's all been a bit . . . frantic.'

'Frantic,' Eden repeated. 'Well, I guess that's one word for it.'

She touched the brake and as they rounded a bend, Cal saw the twinkle of lights in the valley.

Eden took her hand from the wheel and laid it over Cal's.

'I think we made it, Cal,' she said.

'I think we did,' said Cal.

He smiled then because he was glad for her. But part of him was already grieving, because she was the best friend he'd ever had and, one way or another, he knew their friendship would soon be over.

Thirty-Six

At the end of the dirt track the trees thinned out and Eden made a right onto a narrow road before taking a left which broadened out into a junction. They joined a highway with white lines down the centre and when Cal saw the electricity pylons with their wires rising and falling toward the distant lights, he knew that they were at the start of their journey home.

The town was a small, sparsely populated place that had grown up along the side of the road to offer beds to passing travellers and hopeful gold prospectors. Back then the streets and bars had been crowded with people looking to make a fast buck, but nowadays the only gold worth having was a hundred miles further south and you needed a licence to get it. So the town had died a little with every passing year, the young kids shipping out the first chance they got while the old folks sat around trying to figure out why they'd never got around to it themselves.

'That place up ahead looks open,' said Cal. 'Maybe they can tell us where we are.'

Eden nodded.

'I've got twenty bucks in my pocket says the first thing we do is get a coffee and something to eat. What do you say?'

*

Bobby's Bar and Grill wasn't the kind of place that usually stayed open much past midnight, although the regulars always tried to squeeze a few extra minutes in before closing time. Bobby generally allowed them only another quarter of an hour or so to finish their drinks because, although they might not have any place better to go, Bobby's wife was sick and he didn't like leaving her alone upstairs at night.

But tonight was different because Jimmy Simpson's boy had got married and today was the day he was heading up north to work in construction. Jimmy's wife had died last fall, and although Jimmy was proud and happy for the new life his son had made, Bobby had caught the look in his eye when the car drove away and in that look he saw all the football games and fishing trips that would never come again. And because Bobby was a good man, he knew that tonight was not a night for early closing.

'You want another one in there?' he asked, nodding towards Jimmy's glass of bourbon.

Jimmy swallowed the last few drops, wiped his mouth and then slid the glass across the counter.

'You're a gentleman, Bobby,' he said. 'You know that, don't you?'

Bobby smiled and poured another shot.

'Be sure and mention that to Sheriff Jobert,' he said, 'when he turns up asking to see my licence.'

'I wouldn't worry too much about that,' said Frank Roberts, who'd been checking for storm damage on the overhead cables for Montana Power & Light and hoped Jobert wouldn't notice that his ladder was still in place. 'If Sheriff Jobert asks to see anything, it'll be a bottle of malt whisky.'

Bobby chuckled. Frank was right, of course. Sam Jobert had been the town Sheriff for fourteen years, which was plenty long enough to know there was never any trouble at Bobby's place.

Bobby looked at the clock and saw it was a quarter after one. He guessed maybe it wouldn't hurt to share one more beer with the guys before calling it a night.

★

Cal jumped down into the parking lot and slammed the van door shut. There were a couple of cars parked near the entrance and a pick-up at the side with a few beer barrels in the back. The faint sound of country music floated through the open windows, the notes of a steel guitar sliding mournfully behind a woman singing a song about lost love. As Eden followed him in, the smell of stale beer rose from the floorboards, the legacy of a thousand careless drinkers.

Cal could tell right away from the bartender's expression that they weren't the kind of customers he was used to.

He stared at them and his hand came to rest inside the glass he was cleaning, like a small animal settling in for the night.

'Can I help you?'

'We were hoping to get something to eat,' said Cal.

The bartender glanced at the other two men and then back at Cal.

'Ain't you a little young to be out after midnight?' he asked.

It was a fair question. But all the same, Cal was glad they had parked the van a little way from the bar.

Some things were just too complicated to explain.

'We're new to the area,' he replied, not wanting to go into the whole story. 'We went for a walk in the woods and got ourselves lost. And we're pretty

hungry, to be honest. So you know, if you've got anything to eat . . .'

'We'd be real grateful,' Eden added, brushing pine
needles from her sleeve.

The bartender set the glass back on the counter.

'You must have been walking a long time,' he said,
looking them up and down. Cal could tell he wasn't
exactly buying their story. But behind him a row of
cold drinks shone out from the chiller cabinet and
Cal decided he wasn't about to give up on them now.

'You're right about that,' he said, giving the bartender one of his friendliest smiles. 'And most of it
was round in circles.'

Eden stepped up to the bar, took the twenty from
her pocket and slid it across the counter.

'Please,' she said. 'Whatever you've got, we'll be
happy to have it. We ain't fussy.'

The bartender put the tips of his fingers on the
twenty-dollar bill, hesitated for a moment, then slid
it back across the counter.

'I reckon you probably need that more than I do,'
he said. 'Besides, I've got some cold ham and cheese
out back that ain't gonna last much longer in this
heat. Be a shame to waste it.'

Eden smiled.

'Thank you,' she said.

The barman's gaze flicked to Cal and then back to

Eden again. 'I know he's foreign and all, but you both look kind of familiar. Are you sure you're not from round here?'

'Definitely not,' said Eden. 'He's English and I'm from Orange County.'

'You're not famous or anything?'

'I wish,' said Cal.

They sat in the corner next to the jukebox where they couldn't be overheard and Cal tried to ignore the looks from the other two men at the bar.

'Are you sure you haven't been here before?' he whispered. 'The bartender seems to recognise you.'

'Never been here in my life,' said Eden. 'You know what it is, don't you? We've been missing for a couple of days and they've probably been showing our pictures on the news channel or something. Once we've had something to eat, we'll put 'em out of their misery and tell them who we are.'

'And then what?'

'Then we phone the police and we get ourselves home.'

Eden saw Cal hesitate and frowned.

'What? Don't you want to go home?'

'Of course.'

'Well, what, then?'

Cal shrugged.

'Oh please,' said Eden. 'Tell me this isn't about Jefferson.'

Cal didn't reply. He picked up the salt shaker from the middle of the table and set it down again.

'Cal, listen to me. Whatever Jefferson's got coming to him is his own fault. We don't owe him anything. Nothing at all.'

'I know. It's just . . .'

'It's just what?'

'I don't think he's a bad person, Eden.'

'You're kidding me, right? You *are* kidding me.'

'No.'

'He abducted us, Cal. He drugged us, put us in his van and carried out his weird little experiments on us while we were asleep. You think that's a good thing?'

'No. But you don't know what it's like to be alone, Eden. You don't know what it's like to feel desperate. Sometimes life gets so dark that you can't see straight. And when that happens you'll do anything to find your way back to the light.'

Eden put her elbows on the table and rested her chin on her palms.

'Is that how you feel?' she asked.

'Sometimes.'

Cal stared out of the window at the lights and the darkness beyond.

'What happened back there was terrifying. But I

don't believe that Jefferson meant for it to happen. He just wanted his dog back, that's all. And we found it for him, Eden. Even though what he did was wrong, we gave him some light and I feel good about that. And it's the first time I've felt good about anything in a long time.'

'But what about the other stuff? All those things we saw?'

'We need to forget about them, Eden. If we start talking to people about what we saw, we'll never be free of them. We have to try and leave them where they are.'

Eden shook her head.

'We can't do that, Cal.'

'Why not?'

'Because what if he does it again? What if he decides he wants something else and abducts some other kid? And what if next time they don't get away?'

'That's not going to happen.'

'How do you know?'

'Because he found what he was looking for.'

Eden was quiet for a moment.

'And what about you, Cal?' she asked. 'What are you looking for?'

Cal thought of Sarah, lying by his side in the dark of the camper van, wanting to be his mother.

'I'm not looking for anything,' he said. 'Nothing at all.'

THIRTY-SEVEN

The bartender arrived with two Cokes and two plates piled high with thickly cut ham and cheese sandwiches, surrounded by a sea of potato chips. He took a towel from his arm, flicked dust from the table and placed the plates carefully in front of them, as though they were royalty.

'Not often we get visitors around here,' he said. 'Least we can do is look after 'em.'

Eden smiled.

'I'm guessing you must be Bobby.'

The bartender looked at Cal and raised an eyebrow.

'She a detective or something?'

'I read the sign,' said Eden. 'Looks like we definitely picked the right place.'

'I don't suppose there was much picking to be done,' said Bobby. 'There ain't another bar and grill around here for thirty miles. And you won't find many of those open at this time of night.'

'Are you always open this late?' asked Cal.

'Nah,' said Bobby. 'You can blame Jimmy for that.' He looked across at the bar where the thinner of the two men was taking a swallow of whisky. 'Ain't that right, Jimmy?'

Jimmy took the glass from his lips and lifted it up in acknowledgement.

'Bobby'll look after you,' he said. 'Bobby looks after everyone.'

'What he really means,' said Bobby, lowering his voice to a conspiratorial whisper, 'is that I've got "sucker" written across my forehead. Enjoy.'

Cal took a bite of his sandwich and tasted fresh butter and the faint tang of mustard. He waited until Bobby was back behind the bar and then put his sandwich back on the plate.

'Is that what you think of me?' he asked. 'Do you think I'm a sucker too?'

Eden didn't answer right away. She ate a couple of potato chips and then took a sip of Coke, as if she needed to give the question some proper thought.

'You do, don't you?'

'No, I don't,' said Eden. 'But I do think you're trying too hard to find some good in a person who doesn't have any. Which is why, when we finish this meal, we need to phone the authorities and tell them what happened.'

'What? No.'

'Cal, listen to yourself. We're in the middle of God knows where and we've got no idea how to get home. What else can we do?'

'I don't know,' said Cal. 'But it's going to be madness, you know that, don't you? If we tell them what we've seen . . .'

In his mind he saw the flashing lights and the news teams with their satellite vans and microphones, all wanting an exclusive, all wanting to join the feeding frenzy that would gather around them.

'But it's madness already, Cal. That's one genie we're never going to be able to put back in the bottle.' Eden pushed her plate to one side and stood up.

'I know it's going to be tough for a while. But we'll stick together, OK? Whatever happens, we'll help each other through it.'

Cal looked at her.

'At least finish your meal first. There's no rush.'

'I know. I have to go to the bathroom.'

'Oh. OK.'

Cal blushed, glad that the lights were low. When Eden was gone, he ate some more of his sandwich and thought how strange it was to be sitting here in comfort when only hours before he had thought they were going to die. It was odd, he thought, the way the mind adapted to different situations. One minute you were trying to work out the best way to stay alive, the next you were savouring the taste of a ham and cheese sandwich and wondering whether – now that you had finished your plate of potato chips – it was OK to lift a couple from your friend's plate.

Cal was still thinking about that when he realised Bobby was standing next to the table with a couple more glasses of Coke and a plate of oatmeal cookies.

'Strange dessert, I know,' said Bobby, putting the cookies in the centre of the table and replacing the empty glasses. 'But you look as though you could use a little more fuel.'

'Thanks,' said Cal, grateful and embarrassed at the same time. 'Are you sure we can't pay you for this?'

Bobby smiled.

'Maybe someday when you're rich and famous,' he said. 'But until then, I'm not too worried.'

'OK, well . . . thanks again.'

There was an awkward silence for a moment, and then Bobby crouched down so that he was level with the table.

'Talking of famous,' he said quietly, 'I know who you are. I saw your picture on CNN.'

The calmness with which Bobby delivered this information took Cal completely by surprise and he took his hands from the table because he didn't want Bobby to see that they were shaking.

'Listen, you don't have to tell me what happened,' said Bobby, 'but you need to let your folks know that you're OK. Your mom looked pretty worried.'

'She's not my mum,' said Cal.

'OK,' said Bobby. 'Well, whoever she is, she needs to know you're safe.'

Cal looked at the wood-panelled walls, the black and white photographs of loggers and gold-panners and the neat row of horseshoes lined up above the door, and he felt angry because once again he was being told what to do by someone who would never know or understand the things he had seen or the way he felt.

But then his anger turned to sadness because he realised, looking at the men at the bar, that it was the same for everyone; that all the things people said or did were just new ways of pretending that they weren't alone. And whether it was this or the fact that tiredness was catching up with him Cal didn't know, but he suddenly realised there were tears in his eyes so he picked up a paper napkin and pressed it to his face because he was embarrassed and he couldn't do anything about it.

'Hey, come on,' said Bobby, squeezing into the seat opposite. 'You know what? I had a son, just like you.'

Cal wiped his eyes and stared at the beer stains and the scratches on the varnished wooden floor.

'Yeah, that's right. John, his name was. We had our ups and downs of course, same as any kids and their parents. But there was something else too.'

Bobby scratched his chin and shook his head, as if the words coming out of his mouth had taken him by surprise.

'I guess I don't normally talk about this kind of stuff. But when I saw you . . .'

He turned to see if Frank and Jimmy were listening, but they were busy with their own conversation.

'See, my son always had this thought, deep down, that I didn't really love him. Never spoke about it, but I knew it all the same. And you know why he thought that?'

Cal shook his head.

'Because I wasn't his real dad, that's why. I mean, as far as I was concerned I was, but his mom had him when she was young, before I met her. So he always kind of felt that because he wasn't really mine, he would never be good enough for me. But nothing ever really got said. When he was eighteen years old he joined the army, went off to fight in the Gulf and that was it. He never came back. And you know what the worst part is?'

Cal stared at the reflection of the lights in the window and said nothing.

'The worst part is, I never got to tell him he was wrong. I never got to tell him that I loved him.'

For the first time since he had sat down at the table, Cal looked at Bobby directly.

'Why are you telling me this?' he asked.

Bobby shrugged.

'Maybe it's because I recognised the look on your face when I spoke about your mom. Or maybe,' he added, 'it's because I recognised the look on hers.'

As he got up to go, Cal said, 'Just give me a few minutes, OK? Then maybe I'll make the call.'

Bobby nodded.

'Take all the time you need,' he said.

Cal watched Bobby walk back over to the bar and start joking with the other guys and for a moment he found it hard to believe that their conversation had taken place. He felt sorry about the whole thing with his son, sure, but he didn't see what it had to do with him, apart from reminding him that people got hurt the world over.

But then he thought of Jefferson, and remembered that he had done a good thing for him. Maybe that was what life was; just a series of good and bad things and the trick was to try to shift the balance, to try to make the good things outweigh the bad.

There had been no reason for Bobby to give them free food, or to come across and talk about his son. But maybe that was just his way of dealing with the bad stuff. Maybe he believed that if you did enough good things, you could somehow fix the world and make it right.

But where did that leave Jefferson?

Cal knew if the police caught up with him, he would be locked away in prison for a long, long time – maybe even for the rest of his life.

There would be no prospect of the world coming right for him ever again.

And although Cal knew it was stupid, in that moment he saw something of himself in Jefferson, saw how they had both been searching their whole lives for a way of making a world that was wrong become right again. And the more he thought about it, the more he became convinced that he should persuade Eden to leave Jefferson out of it. They could say they got lost in the woods. They could say they stumbled out onto a road and hitched a lift, that they didn't know where they were headed.

And then maybe Jefferson would be able to live the rest of his life out in peace, alone with his dog, and all the dark things would go away because the people who dreamed of them were no longer there.

Pushing his plate away, Cal got up from the table and looked across to the corridor, waiting for Eden to return so that together they could begin to set everything straight.

It was then that he saw the figure, standing in the shadows. It stood with its hands behind its back, watching him. Then it took one hand from behind its back and smiled.

But it wasn't until Cal saw the blood, dripping slowly from the tips of the metal shears, that he finally started to scream.

Thirty-Eight

At the bar, Frank and Jimmy spun round on their stools and Bobby put his drink back on the counter.

'What is it, son?' asked Frank. 'What's the matter?'

But Cal was too afraid to speak; leaning on the table for support, he watched the man make his slow, unhurried progress down the corridor towards him.

Bobby pulled up the serving hatch and stepped through at the same time as the man walked out of the corridor into the bar. The man turned, slowly raising the shears until they were pointing straight at him.

'This doesn't concern you,' he said.

'Damn right it concerns me,' said Bobby, and Cal heard the anger in his voice. 'This is my bar and I want to know what the hell you think you're doing. Coming in here and frightening the kid like that.'

Cal saw that the man was smiling, as if he found the whole thing mildly amusing.

'You want to know what I am doing? Then please – watch, and you will see. But I hope you have a strong stomach. These things have a tendency to become . . .' he opened and closed the blades twice in quick succession '. . . messy.'

'OK, that's it,' said Bobby. 'Either you get out or I'll kick you out myself.'

'You heard the man,' said Frank, sliding off his bar stool and rolling up his sleeves. 'Hit the road.'

The man's smile grew wider, as if this new development was a source of unexpected pleasure.

'You see, Cal?' he said. 'You see how people try and make us do things all the time? *Do this*, *Do that*. It makes us angry, doesn't it? Makes us feel like we just want to kill someone.'

He turned to face Frank, who was striding across the floor towards him.

'Is that what you're going to do?' the man asked. 'Are you going to kill me?'

'No,' said Frank, grabbing him by the lapels and pushing him against the wall. 'First I'm going to kick your ass. *Then* I'm going to kill you.'

Holding the man's jacket with his left hand, he drew back his right fist.

The man giggled, an odd, high-pitched sound like an excited child at a birthday party.

'Hit me!' he squealed. 'Hit me! Hit me!'

'Oh, I'm gonna,' said Frank.

He threw a punch at the man's head, but the man twitched sideways and Frank's fist flailed into empty air.

'Missed!' said the man, still giggling.

Frank swore, let go of the man's lapels and swung two more punches at his face.

'Missed!' said the man, moving from side to side like a metronome. 'Missed again!'

He jerked his knee up hard, the force blowing all the air out of Frank's lungs. Then he flipped the shears up, caught them by the blades and swung the heavy wooden handles at the side of Frank's head, knocking him out cold.

All this in less than five seconds, which was the time it took Jimmy to smash a bottle and come running over with the jagged glass clutched tightly in his hand.

'Hello,' said the man. 'Hello, hello.'

As Jimmy swung the bottle at his throat the man leaned back like a limbo dancer and the bottle swished harmlessly though the air. He brought his body forward again and nodded, eyes glittering, as if it was all part of some enjoyable game.

'Again,' he said enthusiastically. 'Again, again.'

'OK, you asked for it,' said Jimmy, breathing heavily, 'and now you're gonna get it.'

'Hee-hee,' said the man, putting a hand over his mouth and snickering. 'Hee-hee-hee-hee.'

Jimmy set his jaw firm and swung the bottle again, putting all his weight behind it.

'Awww,' said the man, sounding almost disappointed as he moved his head effortlessly out of the way. 'You lose.'

He grinned, then snapped forward like a falling tree and his forehead struck Jimmy on the bridge of the nose, the look of pain and surprise still on Jimmy's face when he hit the floor a couple of seconds later.

Cal remembered how easily he had been able to knock the man over in the forest and guessed he had merely been playing games with him, allowing him to get away so that he would still believe that escape was possible. He saw now that the man had simply wanted to extend the game; to give Cal hope so that the end, when it came, would be even worse.

So it was no surprise when the man neatly sidestepped Bobby's first swing with the baseball bat, snatched up a chair and struck Bobby in the centre of the forehead, sending him crashing through the tables in a clatter of glass.

The man turned back to face Cal and Cal saw that he was no longer smiling.

'On your knees,' he said.

Cal bit his lip and tasted blood. Then, very slowly, he shook his head.

'No,' he said. 'I won't do it.'

The man narrowed his eyes.

'If you disobey me,' he said, 'then everything will be harder. We can do this quickly' – he opened the blades and peered through them – 'or we can do it *slow.*'

He lowered the shears again and moved closer.

'So, which is it to be?'

Cal looked desperately around for a means of escape, but the man was standing between him and the door and Cal had already seen how fast he could move.

'I won't tell you again,' said the man.

Cal knew he could no longer rely upon his muscles to support him; the weight of his bones seemed almost too much to bear.

But then he saw the table next to the window and it seemed like a small chance, a glimmer of light. And as the man licked his lips and walked across the bar towards him Cal jumped onto a chair, scrambled across the table and flung himself fists first through the plate-glass window.

THIRTY-NINE

The glass shattered into a thousand pieces as Cal struck it, spraying across the car park like frozen rain. His mind had gone into panic mode now, ignoring the pain as it focused on the task of keeping him alive.

As he hit the bonnet of the pick-up truck, broken glass rattled across the windscreen and he rolled over the side, slamming into the ground with a thump that knocked the wind out of him. He felt blood on his face and saw dark droplets flecking the broken glass beneath him. He was hurt, he knew that much; knew he should find help, find a way to stop the bleeding. But there was no time; if he stayed here he would die.

Struggling to his knees, he cried out in pain but somehow managed to grab one of the truck's tyres, pulling himself up until he was leaning against the bonnet. He looked at the flickering neon sign above the bar and knew that the dark, unlit road was his only hope. But as he took his first steps across the car park, the window by the door exploded and the man stepped out through a hail of glass, throwing his arms wide as if embracing the night.

'Let's play!' he shouted. 'I spy, with my little eye, something beginning with . . .' he turned and pointed the shears at Cal '. . . C.'

As Cal moved away the man kept pace with him, whispering as he walked. 'Something beginning with . . . something beginning with . . . something beginning with . . . C.'

When Cal was backed up against the van, the man stopped and smiled.

'Can you guess, Cal?' he asked. 'Can you guess what I spy?'

'I can,' called a voice.

The man spun round and Cal saw that Eden was standing with her hands behind her back, lit by the flickering sign above the door.

'Go back inside,' said the man, and Cal could hear the anger in his voice. 'I told you what would happen to you if you interfered again.'

'Yeah, you did,' said Eden. As her shoes crunched across the glass, Cal saw her ripped clothes and the blood on her face. 'You like telling people what to do, don't you?'

'I'm warning you,' said the man. 'Go back inside and stay there.'

'You'd like that, wouldn't you?' said Eden. 'Left all alone to play your nasty little games. Well, I've got news for you, pal. I'm playing too.'

This seemed to cause the man some amusement.

'Oh, you want to *play*, do you?'

He slowly beckoned to her with his left hand.

'Come along then, little girl. Come and join the party. I'm sure we'll have lots of fun.' He turned to Cal and wagged his finger at him. 'Now don't you go sneaking off, you hear me? Don't go disappearing just because my back is turned.'

'I spy, with my little eye,' said Eden, 'something beginning with *C*. Is that right? Is that how it went?'

'Come over here,' replied the man. 'Then we can talk about it properly.'

'I've got a better idea,' said Eden as the man's fingers twitched on the handle of the shears. 'Why don't you ask me the question and then I'll tell you the answer.'

The man considered this for a moment.

'All right,' he said at last. 'But you must understand that if you get the answer wrong, someone will have to pay.'

'Well I guess that's just a risk I'm gonna have to take.'

'Excellent,' said the man. 'So, then. I spy with my little eye, something beginning with C.' He paused and Cal heard his soft, shallow breathing. 'Do you know the answer?'

'Yes,' said Eden. 'It's cartridge. The answer is cartridge.'

The man laughed.

'You are an idiot,' he said. 'Don't you even remember your friend's name?'

'Sure,' said Eden. 'But the answer's still cartridge.'

'Enough of this foolishness,' said the man. 'There is no cartridge anywhere to be seen.'

'Well, I guess that makes me smarter than you, then,' said Eden. 'Cos I can see two of them.'

'Where?' sneered the man, looking up at the stars. 'In the sky, perhaps?'

'No,' said Eden, producing the shotgun from behind her back. 'Right here.'

She tapped each barrel in turn.

'One, two,' she said.

Then she held the gun against her shoulder, closed one eye and squinted along the barrels.

'Now either you walk away from him, or I'm gonna let you I-spy exactly what's inside of 'em.'

As the man let out a frustrated moan, Eden said, 'Get in the van, Cal. Do it now.'

Keeping his eyes on the man, Cal fumbled for the handle and pulled the door open.

The man swivelled his head and stared at Cal, his eyes bright with anger.

'Don't you *dare* disobey me,' he said.

'Take no notice, Cal,' said Eden, her finger tightening around the trigger. 'Just do it. Get in the van.'

But as Cal stepped up onto the footplate, the man came snarling towards him with the shears wide open and his teeth bared like a rabid animal.

There was a loud thump, a bright orange flash and the man twisted into the air, his arms raised like some strange bird as the shears fell from his grasp and skidded beneath the van. Then he hit the ground, rolled over and lay still.

Cal threw himself into the passenger seat just as Eden wrenched open the driver's door.

'Bloody hell, Eden,' he said as she climbed in beside him. 'Where did you get that from?'

'Found it behind the bar.'

Pulling the key from her pocket, she thrust it into the ignition and turned. The engine sputtered, strained for a few seconds, then died.

'Oh come on,' she muttered. 'Don't do this to me now.'

She turned the key again and once more the engine refused to fire.

Kicking the pedals in frustration, she turned the key for a third time and was rewarded by a roar from the engine.

'Yes!' she cried, thumping the steering wheel. 'Thank you!'

Then the side window shattered and a bloodied hand reached through and grabbed her by the throat.

FORTY

'Cal!' she screamed, clawing desperately at the hand that was squeezing her throat. 'Help me!'

Cal grabbed hold of the man's arm and pulled with all his strength, but the arm was all muscle and bone and as Cal leaned across to get some leverage, a fist punched through the shattered window and knocked him back into the footwell. Pulling himself up again, he saw Eden struggling to breathe and knew he didn't have much time.

Through a gap in the seats he saw the wheel brace, still lying where Jefferson had left it. Snatching it up, he twisted round and brought it down hard on the man's knuckles. He heard the crack of bone and the hand briefly slackened its grip before fastening itself to Eden's throat once more. Cal lifted the wheel brace and brought it down again and again until at last the hand withdrew and Eden fell forward onto the steering wheel, choking and gasping for breath.

'Drive!' shouted Cal, flinging the wheel brace as hard as he could through the broken window. 'Eden, you have to drive!'

Eden stared at him, blinking as if she had just woken up from some terrible dream. Then she rammed the gearstick forward, revved the engine and they roared across the car park with the van's tyres squealing in protest. Cal checked the mirror but the man was gone. As Eden headed for the entrance, all he could see was a layer of broken glass and the shotgun lying on the ground outside the bar.

'Are you OK?' asked Cal as she spun the wheel and turned out onto the main road.

'I will be,' said Eden, 'once we've put a few hundred miles between us and that frickin' maniac back there.'

'You shot him,' said Cal. 'I can't believe you shot him and he just kept on coming.'

'I was aiming at his shoulder,' said Eden. 'Next time I'm taking his head off.'

Cal slumped back in his seat and looked at the road ahead.

'Hey,' he said as Eden changed gear and began accelerating, 'don't forget your lights.'

Eden twisted the control on the dashboard and the road was suddenly flooded with light.

'Jeez,' she said, stamping on the brakes. 'What's *that*?'

As the van shuddered to a halt, Cal saw what appeared to be a body in the centre of the road. It was lying in an untidy heap and there didn't appear to be any sign of life.

'I don't like the look of it,' said Eden.

'Could be a hit-and-run,' suggested Cal. 'Maybe we should check it out.'

Eden glanced in the door mirror, scanning the road behind. 'Or maybe we should just keep right on going,' she said.

Cal peered out at the dry scrubland and the empty drainage ditches along the side of the road.

'At least drive a bit closer,' he said. 'See if there's anything we can do.'

'OK,' said Eden. 'But we ain't hanging around.'

She let the clutch out and the van moved forward.

'That's close enough,' she said, applying the brakes. 'We don't want to run him down a second time.'

But as Cal looked at the figure lying in the dust he saw the hood and the pale white hands, twitching beneath the folds of the cloak.

'Back up,' he said. 'Back up now.'

Then the figure rose, turned and pointed through the windscreen. As Eden screamed, more dark shapes began to emerge from the ditches, five, ten, a dozen, slowly gathering and moving down the road towards the van.

'It's them,' Eden sobbed, her hands shaking as she struggled with the gears. 'They're coming for me, Cal. They're coming for me, same as they always do.'

'Just stay calm,' said Cal, although his heart was trying to punch its way out of his chest. He put his hand over hers and helped her guide the gearstick into reverse. 'OK, go,' he said. 'Go, go, go!'

Eden released the clutch and the van shot backwards, narrowly missing the ditch as the wheels spun in the dust.

'Keep it straight!' Cal shouted, clutching his seat as the van swung round in a wide arc.

'I'm trying!' Eden shouted back.

The figures were running now, closing the gap with every step.

Revving the engine, Eden pulled the wheel hard right and they spun back onto the grass verge, stopping an inch from the ditch. But as she fought to find first gear there was a loud thump and Cal looked up to see a figure scuttling across the bonnet. Another landed on the roof and then the door flew open and Cal found himself staring into the glowing eyes of a hooded figure that seemed to have no discernible face, only shadows that writhed and twisted until they became a gaping mouth which bared its teeth and lunged into the cabin with an ear-splitting shriek.

There was no time to think. With the creature tearing at his throat, Cal kicked out hard and then slammed its head in the door with all the strength left in his body. As it thumped down into the dust, another came running full pelt and he kicked the door open again, knocking it backwards.

'Drive!' he screamed as more figures threw themselves at the window. 'Just drive!'

Eden thrust her fist through the broken window and another one dropped from view. Then she spun the wheel and accelerated back in the direction of the bar as two more figures slid off the bonnet, bouncing and rolling to the side of the road. A third continued to grip the wiper blades, pulling itself up towards the windscreen.

'Oh God,' whispered Eden. 'Oh my God.'

She snaked the truck from side to side in an effort to shake it off, but nothing seemed to work.

'All right,' she said. 'Hold on, Cal.'

Pressing her foot to the floor, she accelerated through the gears until the speedometer needle was edging sixty. Then, as they drew level with Bobby's Bar and Grill, she suddenly stamped on the brakes and the figure flew off like a rocket, slamming into a telegraph pole and rolling away into the shadows.

'They're still coming,' she said, glancing in the mirror. 'And we don't have much gas left. The tank's nearly empty.'

Cal looked over his shoulder and saw a mass of dark figures running down the road towards them.

'We have to go back,' he said quietly. 'It's the only way.'

He looked at Eden and saw the fear in her eyes.

'Back where?'

'To Jefferson's place.'

'What? Why?'

'Because that's where it all started.' Cal checked the mirror on his side of the van and nudged Eden with his elbow. 'Come on. Go.'

'So what if that's where it started?' asked Eden as the van pulled away. 'How's that going to help us?'

Cal stared at the dark woods and the mountains beyond.

'Because there has to be some way of undoing this,' he said. 'Jefferson's the only one who can help us to find our way home.'

Eden took a last look in the mirror.

'You'd better be right about this,' she said.

Then she turned the wheel, took a left and soon they were heading back up the mountain track. And

the only light was the glow from the headlights because the sky had clouded over and all the stars were
hidden from view.

FORTY-ONE

'Soon as we've stopped, get out fast and run for the door,' said Cal. 'Those things could be anywhere. At least if we're inside, we've got more chance of seeing them coming.'

'And then what?' asked Eden.

'And then we'll figure something out,' said Cal.

The van skidded around the final bend and before the motor had died they were out and running towards the cabin.

The back door was open, just as they had left it, and the rooms were in darkness.

'Damn it,' said Cal. 'I was sure he'd be back by now. Where's the torch? You had it last.'

'I dropped it on the floor, I think,' said Eden, scrabbling through piles of papers in the dark. 'Are you sure you didn't pick it up?'

'I'm sure,' said Cal. 'Look again.'

'I wouldn't bother,' said a voice.

There was a click from the corner of the room and Cal was dazzled by a light shining in his face.

The torch beam moved across to Eden and as she held up her hands to shield her eyes, Cal could make out the silhouette of Jefferson sitting in the armchair. In one hand was the torch. In the other was a revolver, and it was pointed straight at Cal.

'I already used four bullets on those things out there,' said Jefferson softly. 'You know what that means?'

'No,' said Cal, squinting as the torch beam shone in his eyes again.

'It means I've got two bullets left,' said Jefferson, resting the torch on the arm of the chair so that it cast long shadows across the walls. He pushed open the chamber of the revolver, checked the remaining bullets and clicked it shut. 'Two bullets,' he repeated. 'Ought to be enough, don't you think?'

'Wait,' said Cal. 'Why are you doing this?'

Jefferson smiled but his eyes were lifeless, like water or glass.

'Because you betrayed me, that's why. You killed the only thing I ever loved.'

He shook his head, but when he spoke again it was more in sorrow than in anger.

'I would never have hurt you, don't you see? I

only wanted to bring something good back into this world. But now there is only evil; the evil you did and the evil which came out of your heads. And it's out there looking for you, you know that, don't you? It's out there stalking you, hunting you down.'

'That's why we've come back,' said Cal. 'To ask for your help.'

'You want *my* help?' Jefferson laughed bitterly. 'Give me one good reason why I should help you.'

'Because we didn't kill your dog,' said Eden.

'You shut up,' said Jefferson angrily, pointing the gun at Eden. 'Just shut up with your filthy lies.'

'She's not lying,' said Cal. 'She's telling the truth.'

'Oh yeah? And why should she be any different to all the others?'

The gun trembled in Jefferson's hand as he continued to point the gun at Eden, his finger tightening around the trigger.

'No one tells the truth, Cal. Not the vet who told me she could save my dog. Not the people who pretended to be my friends. Even my own mother lied to me.'

Jefferson wiped his eyes with the back of his hand.

'Do you know what she said to me the day she died? She said if I got a scholarship, she would take me out to dinner and buy me anything I wanted. She promised me, Cal. She *promised*. Any damn thing.

But then she left me, same as everyone else. And she didn't even say goodbye.'

As Jefferson spoke, Cal thought of all the times that he had been let down in his life, of all the times he had believed in something or someone, only to have it taken away from him. But suddenly, he saw that it didn't have to be that way. And in that moment – more than anything else – he wanted Jefferson to see it too.

'But we came back,' he said. 'We didn't know your dog was dead, not until you told us just now. That's the truth. And here's something else that's true, whether you believe it or not: Eden wanted to go back for Tansy. She wanted to save her.'

'You're lying again,' said Jefferson, shaking his head. 'You're lying to protect her.'

'She doesn't need my protection,' said Cal, 'but it's true just the same. Your dog knew something was wrong. And if you ask me, she sensed that our lives were in danger. So when the man came out of his cell, she didn't give a thought for herself. She just took off and went for him.'

Jefferson stared at Cal as the torch beam flickered on the wall behind him.

'The man?' asked Jefferson. 'You saw the man?'

Cal nodded.

'We've brought some bad things into this world

and now it looks as though we're going to have to pay for it. But the truth is, we brought a good thing into the world too. And that good thing was your dog. She died trying to save us.'

Jefferson swallowed, lowered the gun and looked at Eden.

'You really wanted to go back for her?'

Eden nodded.

'I wanted to, but I couldn't.' A pause. 'And I'm real sorry about that. She was a beautiful dog.'

'Thank you,' said Jefferson. He placed the gun on the arm of the chair, put his elbows on his knees and covered his face with his hands. For a few moments there was silence. Then Jefferson took a deep breath and let it out again, long and slow, as if he was reaching some kind of decision.

'I should never have brought you here,' he said. 'I see that now. All the bad things that have happened since then are my fault. I thought I could control everything, thought I could make the world the way I wanted it. But I was wrong, and now it's too late.'

'No it isn't,' said Cal. 'It's never too late.'

'It is for me,' said Jefferson, getting up from his chair, 'but maybe not for you.'

'What do you mean?' asked Eden.

'I saw those things in the forest, the dark things from your dreams, but they weren't interested in me.

It's you they want. And I'm afraid they won't stop until they get you.'

Jefferson took a hurricane lamp from a hook on the wall.

'It's the same with your guy, too,' he said, lighting a match so that the flare of paraffin suffused the room with a warm yellow glow. 'He'll attack whatever stands between him and you, that's for sure, but ultimately it's you that he wants.'

'But why?' asked Cal.

'Because there's a darkness in all of us,' replied Jefferson. 'The only difference is that we've taken yours from your mind and given it life in the physical world. But it's still a part of you, Cal. And it's a darkness that will destroy you if you let it.'

'I don't understand,' said Eden.

Jefferson turned to her.

'Then close your eyes,' he said.

'What?'

'Close your eyes and try to remember the last time you had these dreams.'

'But—'

'Just do it, Eden,' said Cal. 'We may not have much time left.'

'OK, OK. Just give me a minute.'

Eden walked across to the sofa and sat down. She clasped her hands in her lap and closed her eyes.

After a few moments Jefferson asked, 'Are you see-ing them?'

Eden nodded, her eyes still closed.

'I'm seeing them.'

'Good. Now this is important. I want you to try and remember exactly how these dreams end.'

'I don't need to remember,' said Eden. 'I already know. They always end the same way.'

Jefferson nodded, as if this was the answer he had been expecting.

'And how is that?'

Eden opened her eyes and Cal saw the light from the lamp reflected in them.

'They're chasing me through the dark and I'm running away. I'm running through the woods and I can hardly see because it's so dark, but then I come to a house and I can hear their footsteps behind me and they're really close, getting closer and my heart feels like it's about to burst . . .'

Eden's breathing was faster now, the dream be-coming more real to her as she spoke.

'And then?' asked Jefferson. 'What happens next?'

'I run towards the house and the door is unlocked, so I push it open and go inside. But then I hear them outside the house, I can hear them moving and whis-pering so I know that they're out there. And I'm scared because I know they're going to find me. So

I crouch down by the window and make myself as small as possible. I think that if I do this they won't see me, they'll think I've gone somewhere else and they'll move on. But then . . .'

'Yes?'

'Then I hear a noise and it's like a scratching above my head. At first I don't want to look, so I just bury my head in my arms and screw my eyes up tight. But then the scratching becomes a tapping, and although I'm scared I can't stop myself, and I look up at the window. Then the tapping stops.'

'But that's not the end, is it?'

'No. It's not the end.'

Cal looked at Jefferson and saw the gleam in his eyes.

'All right, that's enough,' he said as Eden watched the shadows from the lamp flicker across the wall. 'Can't you see how frightened she is?'

'We have to know how it finishes,' said Jefferson. 'We have to know what the ending is.'

He turned back to Eden.

'There is a moment of relief, yes? For a moment, you believe that you're safe?'

'Yes.'

'And then it happens.'

'Yes. But I don't—'

'Eden, listen to me. I want to help you. But you have to tell me how it ends.'

Eden clutched her hands to her chest and stared at the floor.

'I'm still shaking, but I get up, real slow, onto my knees, and I'm looking out of the window. And then a face appears and the window breaks and suddenly I'm screaming and screaming . . .'

'And then?'

'And then . . . I wake up.'

'Yes!' said Jefferson triumphantly. 'I knew it!'

'What?' asked Eden. 'What did you know?'

'That this is the moment,' said Jefferson, 'the moment when they finally get what they have come for.'

The room was silent except for the soft roar of the hurricane lamp.

'It is the moment of your death.'

FORTY-TWO

Cal saw the look of terror on Eden's face and felt the hairs rise on the back of his neck.

'Are you saying I'm going to die?' Eden whispered.

'No,' said Jefferson. 'I'm saying that this is the moment you die in your dreams. It is the moment that the things which pursue you finally achieve their goal.'

'So how's that going to help us?' asked Cal. 'Because they aren't in our dreams any more, are they? They're out there right now, hunting us down.'

'Precisely,' said Jefferson. 'We know from your dreams that they won't stop until they reach that end point. So the only chance you have is to give them what they want. You have to stop running. You have to let them come here and find you.'

'Are you crazy?' asked Eden. 'If they find us, they'll kill us.'

'They'll try to,' said Jefferson. 'But the truth is, they're going to find you anyway. At least in this way it can be at a time of your choosing. And in this way, I think, it is we who can decide how it ends.'

'How?' asked Cal.

'Let's just say I've always expected that one day the authorities would catch up with me,' replied Jefferson. 'That someday they'd look at their records and discover that I sold my mother's house without paying my taxes and disappeared from their system. They wouldn't like that one little bit. So I figured they'd come along with their trucks and chainsaws, telling me that this land didn't belong to me and that I owed them lots of money. And after this, of course . . .'

Jefferson waved his hand around to indicate the whole sorry mess he had gotten them into.

'So anyways. What I'm saying is, I made provisions.'

'What kind of provisions?' asked Cal.

'You let me worry about that,' replied Jefferson. 'Let's just say that anyone comes around who I don't want to be here, I got ways of dealing with them, OK? And while they're being dealt with, I fixed myself a way out. I'll be honest with you, I ain't had cause to go down there in a long while, but I know where it starts and where it finishes, and that's more than you can say for most things in this life.'

'I don't get it,' said Eden. 'Are you saying we've got to wait here for those things to come and get us?'

'No,' replied Jefferson. 'I'm saying you need to go out there and find them. And when you do, you need to bring them back here.'

'Isn't that dangerous?' asked Cal.

'Life is dangerous,' said Jefferson. 'If you want to live it, you have to take risks.'

'Cal?' Eden moved closer, putting a hand on his arm. 'What do you think?'

'I think,' said Cal, 'that we don't have a choice.'

Eden squeezed his arm and then walked across to the door.

'OK,' she said. 'Let's do it.'

*

The clouds were beginning to break up, but the moon was still hidden. After the brightness of the lamp, Cal's eyes took a while to adjust. But soon the shapes of the forest became clearer, trees looming out of the darkness on either side of the track.

'Do you think your guy will come up with the others?' asked Eden as they walked side by side, following the track around the bend.

'I don't know. Maybe. Depends how bad you messed him up with the shotgun.'

'Not so bad he couldn't punch through the window and try taking my throat out.'

Cal stopped and listened to the wind in the trees. 'Eden, what are we doing?'

'I don't know. You want to go back?'

'More than anything. But like Jefferson said, maybe if we do it his way we get to choose how it ends.'

They had only walked a few more paces when Eden stopped and nudged him.

Something was moving up ahead.

Cal saw the shadows change, then return to stillness.

'Did you see that?' whispered Eden.

'Yeah, I saw it.'

They stood motionless, two statues on a dirt track. 'What shall we do?'

'Keep walking. Just a little way.'

'Cal, no. Please.'

Cal wanted to run. He guessed they were probably going to die. But because he knew Eden was afraid too, it somehow made him stronger.

'Hold on to my arm, OK? Just hold on tight and don't let go.'

'I'm scared, Cal.'

'Just a few more seconds, that's all. When we know they've seen us, we'll make a run for it.'

'Promise you won't leave me, Cal.'

'I promise.'

Cal could see the shapes more clearly now, moving through the trees.

'Call to them,' he whispered.

'What?'

'Call to them. Let them know you're here. Then we can get this whole mess over with once and for all.'

Eden took a deep breath and closed her eyes.

Then she opened them again, let go of Cal's arm and cupped both hands around her mouth.

'Hey!' she shouted. 'Hey! I'm over here!'

Beneath the whisper of the breeze Cal heard a low murmur as the figures gathered at the tree line, their ancient incantations echoing amongst the shadows.

Then they turned and swept up the road towards them.

'Go!' shouted Cal and they ran up the track with their shoes slapping against the hard ground, the rasp of their breath heavy on the night air.

As they rounded the bend, Cal saw the house ahead of them and began to think they might actually make it. He heard Eden cry out, gasping for oxygen as she pushed her body to the limit. Then with a snarl something thumped into his shoulder blades and he was rolling in the dust, grappling with hands that threatened to choke the life from his body.

'Leave,' hissed a voice. 'She is ours now. There is nothing you can do to save her.'

Cal didn't reply; instead he tipped his head back, brought the weight of his body forward and slammed his forehead into the darkness of the hood. There was a sound like a gunshot as the blow hit home and he smelled the sweet, sickening stench of decay. Then the figure fell back and he was on his feet again, grabbing Eden's hand and running for the door.

As they stumbled into the living room, Jefferson slammed the door and drew the bolts across.

'Are they coming?' he asked as Cal fell onto the sofa, gasping for breath.

'Oh they're coming all right,' said Cal. He looked down and saw that Eden was curled up in a ball beneath the table.

'Listen,' said Jefferson.

He turned down the lamp and Cal heard the whisper of voices approaching, coming closer and closer, until at last they seemed to seep through the windows and walls of the house.

'She has to come out and face them,' said Jefferson, nodding towards Eden.

'And then what?'

'And then they can do what they have come to do.'

'Kill her, you mean?'

'They have to reach that point, Cal. After that, we can change things. But if this is going to work, you have to do exactly as I say.'

Cal nodded, then got down on his knees and spoke as calmly as he could.

'Eden. You have to come out and face this.' He reached out and touched her hand. 'It's the only way.'

'No,' said Eden, pulling away. 'I *can't*.'

'Eden, listen to me. If we do this, then it will be over.'

'If *we* do this? You're not the one who has to do anything, Cal. It's me. I'm the one they want.'

Outside, the whispering grew wilder, more agitated.

'I'm frightened, Cal. They're going to kill me, aren't they? They're going to kill me and I don't want to die.'

'I promise you you're not going to die,' said Cal. 'But you have to trust me, OK?'

And although for his own part Cal had never been able to trust anyone, he knew he would do everything in his power to keep his promise. Because in the end, even if it meant dying himself, he would at least have proved to himself that there was someone in this world he could believe in.

'Come on,' he said. 'Take my hand.'

As Eden's fingers closed over his own and he drew her out from beneath the table, Jefferson pushed the sofa back and took a crowbar from beside the stove. He bent down and levered up the floorboards, revealing a square wooden hatch beneath. He opened one of the hatch doors and suddenly the room was filled with the smell of damp earth. Cal saw that there was now a deep sloping hole where the floorboards used to be.

'Tell me again,' said Jefferson as the whispering grew louder, 'how your dream ends.'

'Like this,' said Eden, and Cal could tell she was close to breaking, her nerves shredded by the thought of what was to come. 'I see the shadows, and I hide beneath the window, and then they come for me.'

'Then that is where you must go now,' said Jefferson quietly as dark shapes flitted past the window. 'Kneel by the glass and wait. When they come through, you must both run to the passageway and keep on running until you reach the end of it. When you can go no further, push upwards and you will find yourselves at the edge of the wood. Do you have the keys to the van?'

Eden nodded.

'They're still in there.'

'Good. There's a can of fuel in the back if you need it. But you must drive away as fast as you can. Don't stop for anything, and don't look back.'

'But what about you?' asked Cal.

'I can make my own escape.' Jefferson put a hand on Eden's shoulder. 'Don't worry,' he said. 'Everything will be fine.'

Cal saw Eden swallow, watched the way her hands shook and he thought for a moment that she wasn't going to do it. But then she stood up, walked to the window and knelt down with her hands pressed together and her head bowed as if in prayer.

The whispering grew louder until it filled the whole room, hidden voices seeming to taunt and mock them from every corner. Then the voices stopped abruptly, as if someone had pulled the plug from a radio.

In the silence that followed, Eden lowered her hands and raised her head until her face was level with the window.

She stared into the blackness, waiting.

For a moment it seemed as if nothing would happen.

Then, without warning, two eyes appeared on the other side of the glass, glowing like hot coals, and as

Eden screamed there was a sudden roar and every window in the house shattered into a thousand pieces.

FORTY-THREE

They came like a flood, pouring through the windows as the whispers turned to the snarls of predators that have found their prey.

Jefferson took the first one out with a single shot, the flash from the gun's muzzle lighting up the room as the bullet found its target, sending the dark figure crashing to the floor. The second one was right behind it and although Jefferson loosed off another shot it still managed to seize Eden by the hair, dragging her screaming to the centre of the room. Cal grabbed the crowbar and swung it at the crouching figure, knocking it sideways into the wall.

From all around he could hear the muffled thump of more creatures arriving. He watched Jefferson throw the empty gun at one of them and it scuttled up the wall before hanging grotesquely from the ceiling, clinging to the boards with bony fingers as it surveyed the scene below.

'Run!' shouted Jefferson, pulling Eden up from the floor. But as Eden stumbled towards Cal, the creature released its grip on the ceiling and descended upon Jefferson with an unearthly howl.

As another one came at Eden from the kitchen, she grabbed the hurricane lamp and swung it round in a wide arc, hitting the creature squarely in the face with a loud *crump*.

Cal stepped over it as it fell, raising the crowbar and bringing it down hard upon the head of Jefferson's attacker. As the figure screeched and turned to face him, he looked towards the bedrooms and saw both door handles turning simultaneously.

'Go!' shouted Jefferson as more figures appeared at the windows.

Eden stared at them, unable to move.

'There are too many of them,' she said helplessly. 'It's too late.'

But Cal didn't want to believe that. And so as the bedroom doors flew open he leapt at her, pushing her across the room and throwing her down through the hole in the floor. The momentum carried him after her and together they tumbled down the roughly dug slope to the tunnel below.

As the howls reached a crescendo above him, Cal

scrambled back up the slope saw that the whole room was bathed in a strange yellow light. Jefferson's face was covered in blood and as he ran towards the hatch, Cal slid backwards to let him in. But instead of jumping down into the hole, Jefferson put his hand on Cal's head, pushed him back and slammed one of the hatch doors shut.

'Put the bolt across!' he shouted. 'You have to go now!'

But Cal didn't want to leave him and as Jefferson tried to close the other half of the hatch, Cal put his hands up to stop him.

'No!' Jefferson screamed. 'You've got less than two minutes!' Then because Cal still wasn't moving Jefferson punched him hard in the face, knocking him back into the hole. Wiping blood from his mouth, Cal struggled up again to see two figures dragging Jefferson away from the hatch. Outside, a lone figure watched from the shadows.

'Please,' Jefferson screamed. 'Go!'

In the distance, Cal heard a low rumble and then the rumble became a roar as the slime-covered creature from Eden's nightmares burst through the floorboards, coiling around Jefferson's legs and dragging him down.

'Tansy!' Jefferson screamed, hysterical now. 'Tansy, where are you?'

As more figures swirled around Jefferson's struggling form, Cal slammed the hatch shut and drew the bolt across. And as Cal followed Eden down the tunnel he could hear the sound of bolts loosening and the voices whispering, *We are coming, we are coming* . . .

'This is it,' breathed Eden, stopping suddenly. 'This is the end of the tunnel. We can't go any further.'

'We have to,' said Cal.

The earth sloped up into a solid wall, but as Cal ran his hands across its surface he discovered a step, dug roughly into the soil. The space was narrower here and as he climbed onto the step he had to bend over until his back and shoulders were touching the roof of the tunnel. As he pressed against it he felt it give slightly and, using the strength in his legs, he pushed up as hard as he could. After a moment's resistance, the earth gave way and then he was scrambling out into the forest and above him was the night sky, and the moon, and the stars.

*

Back at the house, Jefferson knew that he was dying. The darkness he had tried to escape from for so long had found him at last, just as he had always suspected it would. But as consciousness began to slip away from him he knew that – perhaps for the first time in his life – he had done a good thing. A last, unselfish act that would mean the girl and the boy would be free.

He stopped struggling then and imagined the two of them going out into the world, living their lives, moment after precious moment.

And as the timer beneath the floorboards ticked away the final few seconds, he closed his eyes and smiled.

'Tansy,' he said. 'I'm coming.'

*

It happened as they reached the van.

There was a deep thump followed by a bright flash and an orange fireball rolled up into the night sky. Seconds later the pressure wave knocked them both off their feet, rattling the windows of the van and rushing through the trees with a roar like a jet engine.

'My God,' said Eden picking herself up from the floor. 'What was *that*?'

It was then that Cal remembered the network of wires he had seen disappearing into the roof void, under the floor and behind the walls of the cabin.

And he remembered the words Jefferson had spoken earlier that evening:

I made provisions. Anyone comes around who I don't want to be here, I got ways of dealing with them.

'He never intended to leave,' said Cal. 'He knew all along he'd have to stay.'

For a while they watched the flames consuming the place where the house had once stood, timbers turning to ash in the fierce, unforgiving heat.

In the morning nothing would remain but the smoke and the dust, and the memories that would try to convince them, years later, that the things they had seen had been real.

FORTY-FOUR

High up in the treetops, caught between two branches, a flat-screen monitor lay on its side. The force of the explosion had ripped it from its stand and – as the roof of the building had disintegrated outwards – lifted it skywards before lodging it delicately on a lattice of pine needles, almost twenty metres above the ground.

Remarkably, the screen was still intact.

Even more remarkable, however, was the fact that the screen was still flickering, as if lit from within.

Scientists observing this strange phenomenon might have pointed out that the capacitors in some pieces of electrical equipment are capable of holding their charge for several minutes after the source of energy has been removed. The more adventurous might even have suggested that the recent thunderstorm was responsible, blaming electronically charged particles in the atmosphere for causing the strange light that sparkled across the screen.

What they might have found harder to explain, however, was the image that appeared. At first it was simply a mixture of colours: greens and blues with the occasional splashes of yellow and red. But then, for a few brief moments, the blue become a summer sky and the greens and yellows turned into a meadow full of flowers.

And in the centre of the meadow, beyond the river where the trout swam in silent pools, a man was running with his dog.

But, of course, no one was there to see it.

After a few moments, the image faded to black.

FORTY-FIVE

The police were all over town, tyres screeching and sirens wailing as they tried to find out why two hundred pounds of high explosive had suddenly blown a hole in the side of their mountain.

Cal and Eden sat in the bar of Bobby's Bar and Grill watching the lights flash past and listening to Sheriff Jobert say, *Well, I'll be damned* for the twentieth time that evening.

'So let me get this straight,' he said. 'This Jefferson fella takes you up there in his van and you lift the keys, jump in and drive it down here. Twice.'

'That's right,' said Cal. 'The first time we were attacked by the guy who'd been following us, so we had to go back up there.'

Sheriff Jobert looked at him doubtfully.

'You know anything about this, Bobby?' he asked.

'Yeah, he was the guy I was telling you about,' said

249

Bobby. 'The crazy guy with the scissors. He was trying to kill the kid.'

'Which is why I shot him,' explained Eden.

Sheriff Jobert sat down and took his hat off.

'You *shot* him?'

'Yeah. I didn't kill him, though.'

'Well, that's something. Where is he now?'

'Don't know. But he's wearing, like, really old-fashioned clothes and he's got a chunk blown out of his shoulder, so he shouldn't be too hard to find.'

'I saw him,' said Frank Roberts, who was sitting at the bar with a bandage round his head.

'Me too,' said Jimmy Simpson, his voice distorted by the plasters taped over his nose. 'Right before he kicked the kahoomas out of me.'

'I don't mean that,' said Frank. 'I mean I saw him afterwards. He was heading out after those other guys.'

'Other guys?' said Sheriff Jobert, scratching his head. 'What other guys?'

Frank shrugged. 'Don't know who they were but there was a whole bunch of 'em. Heading up towards the mountain.'

'So he *was* with them,' said Cal, remembering the figure he had seen outside the window moments before the hatch closed.

'With who?' asked Sheriff Jobert, trying to keep track of the conversation. 'Who are all these people?'

'They were after Eden,' explained Cal. 'They were trying to kill her. Which is why Jefferson did what he did.'

'Hold on,' said Sheriff Jobert. 'So you're telling me that the guy who abducted you blew up his house to save you from a bunch of people who were trying to kill you?'

'Well, they weren't exactly people,' said Eden. 'But you've kind of got the gist of it.'

Sheriff Jobert didn't believe any of it, of course. At least not the part about Cal and Eden being chased up the mountain by a bunch of psychos. He guessed it was some sort of – what did they call it now – *Stockholm syndrome*, where people who have been abducted imagine all kinds of strange things to try to make their captors seem like decent people.

Of course, Frank Roberts said he'd seen them too, but then Frank had been drinking all night. If Frank had said he'd seen a bunch of little green men wearing space suits, Sheriff Jobert wouldn't have been a bit surprised.

'I guess you must be pretty tired,' he said, thinking maybe he should take a look at the crime scene before the Fire Department hosed all the evidence away. 'All right if we put 'em up here tonight, Bobby?

We'll be contacting their folks just as soon as we can, but the campground's several hours' drive away and these two look like they could use some shut-eye before their folks arrive. Whaddya say?'

'Fine by me,' said Bobby. 'Been quite a day, huh?'

Cal nodded, fighting to keep his eyes open. Tiredness was taking over and already the horrors of the last few hours were starting to fade.

Now all he wanted to do was sleep.

'Come on,' said Bobby. 'Let me show you to your rooms.'

The bedrooms were part of a single-storey extension on the back of the bar, built to cater for weary travellers on their way to somewhere more exciting.

'Just a place to get your heads down for the night,' said Bobby, unlocking the doors to reveal identical rooms with tasselled lampshades and candlewick bedspreads. 'We keep meaning to redecorate, but what the hey. I think you'll find the beds comfortable enough.'

When he had gone, Eden paused in the doorway of her room.

'Cal, are you gonna be OK?' she asked.

Cal nodded.

'Really?'

'I will be.' He scratched at the door frame where

the paintwork was starting to flake. 'No one will believe us. You know that, don't you?'

'Yeah, I know. Does it matter?'

Cal shrugged.

'I'm not sure I even believe it myself.'

'It happened, Cal. You saw it. We both did.'

'So what are we going to do?'

'We're going to go to sleep, Cal, that's what we're going to do. And in the morning, when we wake up, that's when we have to decide.'

'Decide what?'

'On whether to tell the whole story and become part of some crazy circus, or whether to just tell the part they'll understand so we can move on with our lives.'

'But we'll know the truth, won't we, Eden? We'll never forget what happened.'

Eden came to him then, put her arms around his waist and rested her cheek against his chest.

'No,' she said. 'We'll never forget.'

They stayed like that for a long time, beneath the pale glow of the corridor lights. Then Cal kissed the top of her head and let her go.

'Well, I guess we should get some sleep,' he said.

Eden smiled.

'Sweet dreams,' she said.

Outside in the car park, Sheriff Jobert studied the holes that peppered the side of the van and concluded that they had been made when the girl fired the shotgun. If her story was true, it would be easy enough for forensics to lift some prints from it. Peering through the side window, he noticed broken glass on the driver's seat and a mattress laid out in the back. Even if the place on the mountain was destroyed, there was enough evidence here to make some sense of what had happened. The abductor might be dead, but his DNA would tell the story and help Sheriff Jobert put this whole thing to bed.

The main thing was, the kids were alive.

Sheriff Jobert was quietly proud of the way he had dealt with such a major incident. It had only been a couple of hours, but the fire crews were busy dousing the flames and he was already starting to think up a little speech for the news crews who would come flocking in the morning.

I think you'll find we've pretty much got this thing wrapped up, he would tell them. *There ain't too much gets past Sheriff Jobert.*

Which, while generally true, didn't reflect the reality of the current situation.

Because, as he walked across the car park to his

patrol car, Sheriff Jobert failed to notice either the dark figure clinging to the underside of the van's chassis or the steady drip of blood that was already forming dark pools on the tarmac beneath.

FORTY-SIX

Although he was exhausted, Cal found it hard to fall asleep. The adrenalin rush of the last few days had left his mind spinning and every time his eyes were about to close, the images would return: the dark figures climbing through the window, Jefferson trying to close the hatch as they tore into him and – perhaps the most disturbing of all – the shadow of the tall figure and the glint of steel, glimpsed through the window moments before the glass shattered.

Had he imagined it?

He didn't know.

All he knew was that Eden had faced her demons and her demons had been destroyed.

But what of his?

As he stared at the shadows on the ceiling, cast by the night light that he couldn't bring himself to turn off, he thought back to the evening before everything happened. Michael saying, *You should let her make breakfast for you once in a while.* Cal telling him he could look after himself. And Michael saying, *I know, but you don't have to. Not any more.*

Cal thought of Jefferson, of Bobby and his son, and of how it had been too late for them. He thought of Sarah, lying next to him on the bed as he woke from his nightmares.

And Cal knew then that he had been wrong all these years, pretending he could walk through this world alone. He saw that he had been wandering in dark woods all of his life.

But now he had been given a chance.

A chance to walk out of the darkness into the light.

> Star light, star bright
> First star I see tonight
> I wish I may, I wish I might
> Have the wish I wish tonight

Cal felt a stirring of hope and, for the first time in years, he didn't try to shut it away. Because if bad dreams could come true then maybe – just maybe – there was some hope for the good ones too.

Climbing out of bed, he pulled back the curtain to look at the stars. But the glow from the night light meant all he could see was his own reflection. It was the first time he had seen himself for a while and he realised how tired he looked. There were dark rings beneath his eyes and his shirt was stained with blood.

But he was alive, wasn't he?

He was alive, and tomorrow was another day.

It wasn't until he lay down on the bed and switched off the light that he heard the soft *tap, tap, tap* at the window. Hardly daring to move, Cal turned his head and saw, standing on the other side of the glass, the silhouette of a man in a long frock coat.

In one hand he held a top hat, covered in blood.

In the other hand was a pair of scissors.

As Cal watched in horror, the man slowly opened the blades, closed them again and tapped three times on the window.

Then he smiled and mouthed two words through the glass:

'Hello, Cal.'

FORTY-SEVEN

Cal reacted fast, tiredness evaporating as he wrenched the door open and raced down the corridor. He knew if he could just get to the bar and find Bobby or Sheriff Jobert then maybe they would have their shotguns or whatever it was they carried.

But when he opened the outside door, the bar lights were out and Sheriff Jobert's car was gone.

And standing less than ten yards away, in the middle of the car park, was the man with the scissors.

'It's over, Cal,' he said, and Cal saw that he was no longer smiling. 'Don't you see? It was over the moment you brought me into the world. And now it is time for the running to stop. It is time for you to embrace the darkness.'

Cal knew it was hopeless now, knew that by the time help came it would be too late. But in the last few moments he had caught a glimpse of the future, seen how things might turn out, and he couldn't turn away, not now, not when it was so close.

'No one loves you, Cal,' said the man, walking towards him. 'But that's why you created me, isn't it? Because I can take away the pain. The pain of knowing that no one cares about you, that you are all alone in the world.'

'No,' whispered Cal. 'It isn't true.'

'Yes it is, Cal. In your heart, you *know* it is.'

'Maybe I did once,' said Cal, backing away. 'But not now. Not any more.'

The man quickened his pace.

'Don't you run from me,' he said. 'The game's over, do you understand? It's time to finish it.'

But Cal was thirsty for life in a way he had never been before, wanting to unwrap the secrets that lay hidden in the months and years ahead.

So he took a deep breath of sweet, life-giving oxygen.

Then he began to run.

'No!' screamed the man. 'No! No! No!'

A light came on in the annexe.

But Cal kept on running, across the car park and out onto the open road, running the way he had come, towards the mountains and trees and the path which would lead him back to the dark woods once more.

The man was close now, getting closer. Cal heard how easily he ran, long legs striding across the dusty road as his shoes ticked out a regular rhythm, a clock counting down the last seconds of life.

And as Cal ran down the slip road where the electricity pylons crouched beside the drainage ditches on the edge of town, he knew he could never outrun him. He saw the woods looming in the distance and realised he didn't want to run in darkness any more.

Life is dangerous. If you want to live it, you have to take risks.

With a single leap, Cal crossed one of the ditches and ran beneath the power lines toward the ladder that Frank had left fastened to one of the pylons. There was a block of wood halfway up to deter any would-be climbers, but Cal was driven by fear and he quickly pulled himself over it before continuing his upward climb.

In less than a minute he had reached the top of the ladder, but the man was already climbing after him. The gap between the metal stanchions was quite wide, but by pulling himself up on the central struts, Cal was able to make reasonable progress. As he climbed higher, the gaps lessened and he was able to climb more quickly.

He heard the regular clang of metal from below as

the man continued to climb after him, but he didn't bother to look back.

He just kept on climbing, higher and higher, and as he climbed he saw the silhouettes of trees and mountains stretching up towards the very edges of space.

As he climbed up and up his arms ached until the pain was almost unbearable, but it was nothing now compared to the ache he felt inside as he looked up at the stars. Because here, in these final few seconds, he was climbing out of the darkness at last, climbing towards the light, and in his heart he knew that this was what he had been trying to do all his life.

'It's no good, Cal. This is the end, do you hear me? It is time to finish it.'

With a sob, Cal climbed out onto the arm of the pylon and then he was under the power lines that swooped away into the night, and there was nowhere left to go.

Star light, star bright

'That's right, Cal . . .' the man whispered.

First star I see tonight

'No more games now . . .'

I wish I may, I wish I might

'Look at me, Cal . . .'

Have the wish I wish tonight

'See how I make your dreams come true . . .'

Cal felt a sharp pain in his calf and as he cried out the man gave a long, trembling sigh. Cal looked down and saw that the man had slashed at his leg with the shears and the blades were dark with blood.

'You see how painful life is, Cal? How much *suffering* there is in the world?'

Cal turned his head away.

'No, Cal. Look at me. *Look* at me.'

Cal felt the blades press against his cheek and saw that the man was level with him now, one hand gripping the metal struts of the pylon, the other holding the shears.

'You dreamed me, Cal, remember? You dreamed me and that's why I'm here.' His voice was softer, almost tender now. 'But you know that already, don't you? I'm here to take your pain away at last, Cal. I'm here to make your dreams come true. All you have to do is hold out your hands.'

Cal turned his face away and looked at the stars, more beautiful than he ever remembered.

Behind him, he heard the creak of the shears opening.

'Give them to me.'

Cal gripped the metal pylon with one hand and slowly held out the other. He knew now that the stars were just illusions, just like all the times he'd believed that someone in this world might actually care whether he lived or died.

'All right,' he said, and when the shears creaked open a little more, he closed his eyes because it was more than he could bear. 'Just do it.'

But then, from somewhere far below, he heard a scream.

'Get away from him, you crazy freak! Get away from him *now*!'

Cal opened his eyes and looked down to see Eden, standing with a rock gripped tightly in her hand.

'You're too late,' sneered the man. 'He belongs to me now.'

Eden pulled back her arm and threw the rock so hard that it almost reached them, falling away at the last moment to strike the metal frame with a clang.

'All right,' she called, 'I'm coming up.'

As Eden started to climb, the man watched her for a while and then turned back to Cal and smiled.

'By the time she gets here, my work will be finished. But I look forward to showing her how it is done.'

'Please,' said Cal as he understood what the man was saying. 'It's me you've come for. You don't have to hurt her.'

'I know that,' said the man. 'But the thing is, you see, I *want* to.'

Cal watched Eden reach the top of the ladder and pull herself onto the metal framework before continuing to climb, slowly, steadily, almost certainly knowing that she would probably be too late and that she would lose her own life too.

But she kept on climbing anyway.

And as Cal watched her he realised that although some stars might be an illusion, others were real. That even when the sky was so full of clouds that you couldn't see them, there were still stars up there, waiting to be found.

And as the man opened the blades for the last time, Cal drew back his leg and kicked him with all the hatred and strength and love that was left in his body.

His foot struck the man's arm directly beneath his elbow and Cal saw a momentary look of surprise on his face as his hand flipped backwards, the shears still gripped tightly in his fist. As the man struggled to regain his balance, Cal looked into his eyes and saw that he was afraid. Then, as he reached out with his other hand to steady himself, there was a crackle of electricity, a flash of light and a high-voltage spark traced a line through the air, jumping from the power cable to the tip of the shears and through the metal blades into the centre of the man's body.

With an ear-piercing scream the man arched his

back, jerking and twisting as a hundred thousand volts ripped through his veins like summer lightning. As his skin sizzled and burned he released his grip and tumbled backwards off the pylon, an eerie blue light dancing in the air all around him. Then, as Cal turned his face away, there was a blast of heat and the man exploded in a white-hot fireball which blew him into a million pieces.

*

When Cal finally found the strength to climb down again, Eden was waiting for him at the base of the pylon.

For several minutes, neither of them spoke.

They watched the last of the glowing embers fall from the sky, their orange fires fading and turning to ash. Then, as Eden put her arms around him, Cal looked away to the east and saw that the sky was lightening and that soon it would be morning.

As the sun edged its way above the mountains, he took Eden's hand and together they crossed the ditch, walking back down the main street towards Bobby's Bar and Grill, where soon the whole world would be turning up, wanting to know what had happened.

But for now, the world could wait.

Because Cal was busy thinking about how he would ask Bobby if he could set up one of the tables in the bar.

He would put out some plates and bowls, fry a little bacon maybe, fix up some strong coffee.

He remembered how Sarah had lain on his bed that night, holding his hand in the dark before all this madness began.

You should let her make breakfast for you once in a while, Michael had said.

And so he would.

But this time, just this first time, he was going to make it for her.

Because – well – it was a pretty bad job if you couldn't make breakfast for your own mother once in a while.

As they walked across the car park towards the front door, Eden turned to him and smiled.

'It's over, Cal,' she said. 'You realise that, don't you? It's finally over.'

And Cal shook his head and smiled back at her.

'No,' he said. 'It's just beginning.'